MW01632338

The characters and events in *Art and Artifice* are fictitious. Any resemblance to real events or to persons living or dead is entirely coincidental.
Except for the thing about the two-year-old menace. That was definitely a real dude.

First Edition

Published by the author with the assistance of Integrity Reprint Publishing.

ISBN 978-1-7380662-1-6

Art & Artifice

Art & Artifice

A NOVELLA

BY

Owen Hebbert

Niagara, Ontario
2025

"Your name?"

"Roy Lancaster."

"And you have an appointment."

"I do. I am here to meet Dudley Peterkin."

The young man behind the desk glanced over the top of his computer screen with a brief flicker of curiosity. He looked back at the screen.

"You're early."

"Yes."

"Can I get you a beverage while you wait?"

"I'm not that early."

He nodded. "I'll take you up."

The anteroom outside Dudley Peterkin's office was a walk-in resumé, with the man's successes carefully arranged for viewing.

"You may take a seat while you wait," said the receptionist.

"Thank you." I remained standing.

He nodded and left.

I slowly made my way around the room, inspecting each display in turn. The first item on my tour was a photograph of a rugby team wearing MIT colours, with a very young, lanky Dudley kneeling in the front row and holding a silver trophy salver. On the wall next to this was a framed ALT Pass card, a credit card–sized piece of plastic representing a staggering logistical achievement that had simultaneously reduced airline waste and the cost of flying worldwide. There was a large concept drawing of the Pelican, Dudley Peterkin's elegant public transit system, which promised to revolutionise commuting, community building, and urban planning for generations to come. Next to this was a photograph of the first operational Pelican Station, based on the revised Pelican II, in a town outside Portland. On a small pedestal stood the first generation Keen, a little rust-coloured rectangle that had dramatically redirected the smartphone industry away from disposability and toward recyclable, upgradeable hardware. A photograph of a shimmering coastline celebrated the suite of green energy technologies centred around harnessing the ocean's tides that Dudley Peterkin had been working on for almost fifteen years.

I had done my research and recognised these monuments as highlights of a remarkable career. Starting any one of these enterprises would be a staggering accomplishment, yet Dudley Peterkin was behind every single one of them.

I looked about me with feelings of excitement and trepidation. The one area where my research had done nothing for me had been in revealing particulars of Dudley Peterkin's personal life. Somehow, he had managed to remain beyond the reach of celebrity culture. In the vacuum left by his inordinate love for privacy was a swamp of rumours and conspiracy theories that variously romanticised his career or else described him as a dangerous villain who wielded unlimited wealth and influence in pursuit of personal agendas.

The door through which I had entered the anteroom opened and in walked Amelia Peterkin. I recognised her bright blue eyes and amused smile immediately, but the few photos I had seen of her did no justice to her beauty. She was tall—easily as tall as I was—and her curly, chestnut hair was short, which served to exaggerate her height. The moment she entered the room, she made eye contact with me and smiled. There was something about her ready confidence and quick friendliness that was utterly disarming. I felt boyishly shy.

"Hello!" she said cheerfully.

I dipped my head respectfully. "Good afternoon, ma'am."

Amelia passed through the anteroom and opened the door to Dudley's office without knocking. She vanished, shutting the door behind her.

I stepped closer to the picture of the rugby team. The image didn't seem to fit among the mementos of greatness around it. Who, in ranking their accomplishments, would place a college rugby win alongside society-revolutionising technologies like the Keen?

"Hi there!"

I turned. The man himself was leaning out of his office. "Roy Lancaster? I'm Dudley. Why don't you come in?"

I followed him into the office, and he shut the door behind us. The room was large but disordered. The primary piece of furniture was a conference table which he seemed to be using as a desk. The walls and shelves were bare, and in the corner was a pile of cardboard boxes.

Amelia was standing by the conference table and smiled warmly at us as we entered.

"This is my wife, Amelia," said Dudley. "Amelia, this is Roy Lancaster."

"I thought that might be you," said Amelia. She offered her hand, and I shook it. Her handshake was firm but brief. "As soon as I saw you, I thought, *That looks like a butler!"* Amelia spoke with an accent that was subtle and hard to place. It was clearly English at its core, but she seemed to have onboarded the friendliest tones and inflections of other regions. You sometimes hear this sort of accent from people who move around a lot as children.

"It's a pleasure to meet you," I said.

"The pleasure is all ours," said Dudley, shaking my hand in turn.

The enigmatic billionaire was more handsome and agreeable than I had expected. He was lightly built and of average height, which made him an inch shorter than his wife. Like Amelia, he made eye contact very easily and smiled up at me with an open earnestness. He possessed the undisguised good humour, wide eyes, and plain speech of a child.

"Is this a new office?" I asked, indicating the boxes in the corner with a tilt of my head.

"No," said Dudley. He waved me into a seat. "You're joining us at a very exciting time, Mr. Lancaster."

"Oh yes?"

Dudley smiled at Amelia, and she beamed back at him. They looked very happy.

The day I met Dudley Peterkin was the day he vacated his role at Pet Projects, the seat from which he had long directed his companies and research. He and Amelia had agreed that as soon as he "made it," he would turn his business affairs over to younger, more ambitious persons. Their shared vision was of leading a quiet, idyllic life together in a country house.

That's where I come in. I can't pretend to know when Dudley Peterkin first decided that this scheme should involve buttling, but to the romantic imagination of that young man, a butler was as essential to Paradise as jugs of wine and loaves of bread had been to the poet. There were other comforts that the Peterkins planned for this new season of their life—a slower pace, beautiful gardens, and more time spent together—but the butler was never absent.

When I entered Dudley Peterkin's office in late November of 2019, I unknowingly did so as a symbolic character. To call me a trophy is demeaning, I suppose, and not quite accurate. I was a destination at which he had arrived, the picture that is made when a puzzle is assembled. His pursuit of enduring success and inordinate wealth had always been a long shot, and yet here stood a butler. To Dudley's eyes, my greying temples, firm posture, and civil formality perfectly mirrored the butler of his dreams. Clearly, he had made it at last.

*   *   *

A little over two years later, on February 19, 2022, Dudley Peterkin attended a charitable event in New York where a viewing of several underexposed artists was arranged to draw donors. Dudley Peterkin harboured no interest whatever in art, but the charity being supported was one in which he was deeply invested.

After he left his company behind, Dudley turned his analytic and problem-solving genius to philanthropy. Between his personal fortune and the stipend issued to him by Pet Projects, he sported deep coffers from which to give, and the challenge that excited him in this new enterprise was figuring out where his money would have the greatest effect. He studied charitable opportunities like an investor seeking the best rate of return. He didn't particularly care what the giving opportunity was, if he knew it would have a significant effect. Consequently, buying a child a wheelchair could be as exciting to him as building a hospital.

The charity he was supporting on this particular evening was one that Dudley had started himself. He had been looking into the impact of building schools and found that in some remote locales, a school building didn't make sense. Sometimes the local population was too scattered to send their children to a central facility, and sometimes families couldn't afford to have their children attend regularly because they were essential to their household economy. Dudley's solution was to sponsor regional networks of travelling teachers that could bring basic education to families or family clusters.

It was while helping the event's hostess schmooze a particularly reluctant donor that Dudley happened to glance up and see a woman peering over the top of her smartphone at him. Based on her skin tone, her expression, and the greyness of her eyes, the woman was dead. She stood frozen; her colourless, gaunt figure posed with the awkward inflexibility of a corpse. Dudley stared at her in mesmerised horror. There was something about her mute expression combined with the severe disorder of her appearance that arrested his attention entirely.

Beside the woman was a man, also lifeless, also clutching a smartphone. In his ear was a wireless earpiece. He and the woman seemed to be looking past one another completely, as if incapable of seeing anything at all. Behind the man was a dark hellscape—all red earth, ragged stone outcroppings, and ominous black pools—riddled with grey-white corpses. Behind the woman was a garden filled with exotic birds, abundant sunshine, and happily dancing men and women—all with the pallor and grace of the dead.

"Excuse me," said Dudley to the hostess, breaking away from the tedium of selling virtue to the wealthy.

He crossed the room, approaching the two figures who had caught his attention. They were composed of oil upon a single giant canvas that was divided into two distinct halves. He drew to a halt about ten feet from the painting and studied them again, trying to identify what it was that drew him. There was no beauty in the figures to attract him, yet he could not look away.

"Deep in thought?"

Dudley started and turned to find a small, middle-aged man standing next to his elbow. The man was dressed all in black and was clutching a glass of red wine. Both his attire and his features gave him a severe, artistic appearance. His dark hair was buzzed close to his scalp, and from his thin hands sprang long, knobby-knuckled fingers. One of his narrow eyebrows was raised like a question mark as he smiled up at Dudley, exaggerating the hollow, boney appearance of his face.

"Hi," said Dudley, looking back at the painting. His eyes remained busily at work unpacking the painting and its myriad elements. "I'm just taking it in."

"Do you like it?" the little man asked.

"I don't know yet," said Dudley with his customary candour. He caught himself and glanced at the other apologetically. "Sorry," he said. "Is it yours?"

The man smirked, amused at Dudley's plain speech and clear discomfiture. He had a mouthful of wine when Dudley addressed him, and he took his time swilling it before swallowing and nodding. "Yes," he said shortly. He gestured along the wall on which a whole array of similar works was displayed. "These are all mine."

"I don't know anything about art," said Dudley. "I hope I didn't seem critical."

The man waved a dismissive hand that bestowed forgiveness with papish condescension. "Forget it," he advised. "My work is not immediately easy to like. It's not supposed to be."

"Oh," said Dudley. He could not imagine why one would deliberately create work that was not likable. He cast about for something clever to say. "What is it called?" he asked. "There's no nameplate."

The man leaned back to achieve a better view of his own masterpiece. Into the hand that did not hold his wine he rested his chin. "That's a very good question," he said. "The trouble is..." He took a deep breath and then paused, measuring up Dudley as if trying to decide how in-depth he ought to go.

Dudley stared back at him expectantly, his round, agreeable face open and unaffected. He wore the expression of a receptive pupil, listening only to learn.

The artist nodded sagely, apparently satisfied with what he saw. Perhaps he thought this an opportunity to share in the most altruistic way that any of us teaches—to see the other bettered by the wealth of wisdom or knowledge that we possess. It is entirely more likely that he thought this an opportunity to stroke his ego at the expense of someone who would offer no resistance or correction. He extended his hand.

"Lucifer Tremblay," he said.

"Ah!" Dudley shook the offered hand with a friendly smile. "Your name is Lucifer?"

"You may call me Lucy if you prefer," said the strange little man, acknowledging the absurdity of neither.

Dudley did not prefer. He bit his tongue, resisting the urge to ask further questions. Surely this person had not been named Lucifer by an actual mother. Or maybe he had been? It seemed unlikely.

And I will here interrupt my own narrative to confirm that this was, as Dudley immediately suspected, a pseudonym. I will not indulge such an absurd and perverse affectation by my own pen and when referring to the artist will choose to use his given name wherever possible. His given name, as we all learned with a little Internet sleuthing, was Lucian.

Lucian was smirking again as he observed Dudley's reaction to his name. Making "normies" uncomfortable was a weakness of his. "And *your* name?"

"Oh!" said Dudley. He shook his head, embarrassed. "Sorry. My name's Dudley."

"Dudley Peterkin?" The man drew back a little, like a cat who has been teasing a mouse only to suddenly realise that the mouse is the tip of a lion's tail.

"Yeah."

"It's a pleasure to meet you." Lucian spoke with reluctant respect. "I guess I should be thanking you for making this evening happen."

Dudley shook his head, a gentle lion. "No, no," he said. "I don't know the first thing about art, I'm afraid. I wish! No, I just provided the money. That's my strong suit."

"That's fine. I appreciate your money if not your expertise," said Lucian. His smirk had returned as had his calm, reassured by Dudley's eager self-deprecation.

“You were going to tell me about the painting’s name,” said Dudley.

“Its title,” said Lucian. “Naming paintings, Dudley, is a part of the creative process that has always mystified me. Some of my works, like that one over there—I call it *Withdrawal* for obvious reasons—are easy to name. Others…” he gestured to the painting before them with a sigh. “Others refuse to be reduced to a word or two. They capture a reality—an experience or situation or narrative or complexity—that resists summary. That makes no sense to you, does it?” This last sentence was structured like a question but pronounced as an observation.

“I think I see what you mean,” said Dudley.

“Do you?” the man sighed again as if despairing.

“I think so,” said Dudley. “Because the title is a sort of message or a description, isn’t it? Like a key to unlocking what you’re looking at. It has to be just right, and the more complex the painting, I guess, the harder it is to get precisely the right name to trigger exactly the right ideas. Is that…? Is that sort of what you mean?”

“You’re kind of getting it,” said Lucian with a resigned shrug. Of course, it was beyond his strength to concede that Dudley had described the matter perfectly. “You’re a married man, Dudley?”

“Yep!” said Dudley, grinning affably. This was a subject on which he was always happy to speak.

“And how’s that for you? Good? Bad? Had any struggles? Any infidelities? Any heartbreak? Any triumphs? Is your love passive? Passionate? Leisurely? Energetic? Steady? Episodic?”

Dudley, his eyebrows raised in the smallest hint of indignation at this explosion of trespass upon the privacy of his marriage, quickly opened his mouth to answer.

"No," said Lucian, raising a hand imperiously. "Hang on. You may answer all of that, but it must only be with a single word or a single phrase. Nothing more. No paragraphs. No essays of sentiment. A single word or brief phrase is all you have to work with."

Dudley closed his mouth and smiled forgivingly at the illustration. "Mmm!" he said.

"There," said Lucian with almost maternal gentleness. "Now you see, don't you? I can't name this painting any more easily than you can name your marriage. Is it impossible? I'm sure it's not, but I haven't yet discovered the right combination of sounds."

"Well," said Dudley, forming his next thought with self-conscious care, "I guess I have a rare advantage then, because I can get the artist himself to explain everything that would normally be captured by the name—the title, I mean."

"That's nicely put," said Lucian, "but I must decline." He waylaid a waiter to refresh his wine and sidled just a little closer to Dudley. "I'm dying to know more about you, Dudley."

"Me? No, no."

"Yes you."

"That's not as interesting a topic as you might think."

"I think you're wrong. As reclusive as you are, Dudley Peterkin, you have a reputation. You're allegedly a genius. You're allegedly a billionaire.

You're allegedly terraforming the planet. You're allegedly in league with the lizard people."

Dudley smiled to himself. "Yes. I've heard all these allegations before."

"So imagine my surprise when I actually get to meet the man himself, and he's not driving a flying car or curing cancer or shedding his skin. Imagine my surprise when I find him engaging in art analysis."

"Hey now," said Dudley. "Hardly that. I'm just curious."

Lucian pressed on. "It's a side of the man the world has never seen. A patron of the arts. A mind that is capable of saving the planet, founding charitable organisations, *and* grappling with the mysteries of the universe as they are expressed through art."

Dudley laughed awkwardly.

"Don't be shy," said Lucian. "It's a side of you that the public should know about. As far as anybody knows, Dudley Peterkin has completely neglected the arts. It's your best-kept secret, and one you could stand to reveal to the world. It would give your public image a certain..." Lucian stepped back and examined his subject through narrowed eyes. "A certain *panache.* Besides. The art world can always use a rich person who understands why our work is important. Someone like you."

"That's food for thought," said Dudley patiently.

"You think I'm wrong?"

"Maybe."

"You know best," said Lucian with a sigh.

"Would you like to tell me more about this painting?" Dudley asked.

"As you wish."

* * *

The fundraiser was held Saturday evening. Dudley returned late Sunday, and I didn't see him until breakfast on Monday. The Peterkins, in seeking a new life where they could fulfill their dreams of peaceful privacy, chose to purchase a home far removed from the beaten track. The fact that they were a long drive from the nearest city never seemed to bother my employers.

The historic residence at Number Two Harper's Lane contained a secret bubble of simple, tidy living that perfectly reflected the loves and joys of Amelia and Dudley. As I was their butler, that bubble was mine to maintain.

The first I heard of Lucian Tremblay was when the Peterkins were at breakfast Monday morning. I was not, of course, dining with them, but rather standing by the sideboard, serving them.

I employed an outstanding cook, but not for the purpose of preparing breakfasts. That was something I was entirely capable of handling, especially as my employers had the most pedestrian tastes in breakfast food. Paige didn't need to come in early just to make eggs and coffee. I could easily fold breakfast into my morning routine, especially since the Peterkins kept very regular hours.

The conversation about Lucian began with an innocent inquiry by Mrs. Peterkin regarding the success of Saturday evening's fundraising.

"It was great," said Dudley, rearranging the eggs and potatoes on his plate with his fork. I could tell that he wanted to say more, but he was unsure of how to go about it.

Amelia Peterkin also recognised hesitation in her husband's manner.

"Okay?" she prompted. "Did you have any success with the donors?"

"For sure," said Dudley. "We did fine."

"And?"

"And I met a really interesting guy there. He's an artist."

Amelia cocked her head, considering this before reacting verbally. I might have guessed what she was thinking. Her husband was not someone who seemed in any way infatuated by art. If anything, the topic usually made him nervous, as does any subject on which one is embarrassed of one's ignorance. How he'd found this man—this artist—"really interesting" was not easy to imagine.

"Oh?" said Amelia at last.

"His name was Tremblay," said Dudley. "I talked with him the whole evening. Well, almost all of it."

"What about?" The question was delivered with a laugh from his wife.

"His paintings," said Dudley. "I learned a lot."

"Let me look him up," said Amelia. Her phone was on the table next to her, and she grabbed it and tapped deftly through to her browser. Her thumbs hovered, poised above the screen. "What was his name again?"

"Umm," said Dudley as if trying to remember. He reddened a little. "Tremblay." He spelled it out. "His name is Lucifer Tremblay."

Amelia stopped typing and looked up at him. "What?"

"I know!" said Dudley. "That can't be his real name, but it's definitely what he goes by. He said I could call him Lucy!"

"What did you call him?" She was laughing again.

"Neither! I didn't really need to. We were talking to each other the whole time, and I didn't need to introduce him, thankfully."

"Lucifer... Tremblay..." Amelia's expression as she typed his name into her phone was one of pretty amusement. "Okay," she said, clearing her throat as she prepared to read. "Lucifer Tremblay. Painter, philosopher, visionary."

"What are you reading from?" Dudley asked.

"His LinkedIn."

"Does it have a picture?"

Amelia turned her phone so he could see.

"Yeah," said Dudley. "That's him."

"Okay then," said Amelia, resuming her study of the phone. She read aloud, "...capturing the soul of modern humanity through a stylised lens inspired by the Flemish Primitives of the fifteenth and sixteenth centuries."

"That's what he was explaining to me," said Dudley eagerly. "He has this whole thing about how the new millennium needs a new renaissance."

"Oh yes?" Amelia put her phone down and smiled at her husband while folding a piece of bacon several times over.

"Yes," said Dudley. He still seemed bashful. He opened his mouth to speak and then closed it again. "I don't explain it as well as he does."

"That's all right!" said Amelia quickly. "I think it's fantastic that you were able to connect with this guy. Art is normally outside your area of expertise, but you seem to be expanding that horizon nicely. You never fail to amaze."

"Don't give the relationship your full endorsement just yet," said Dudley awkwardly. "I've had a very unusual idea."

"Oh?" Amelia lowered her fork but raised an eyebrow.

"This guy is not making it as an artist. He told me that he sells one or two paintings a year, and the most he's ever sold one for is eleven thousand dollars."

"That sounds about right," said Amelia. "Most artists need a day job, you know. Frankly, it sounds like he's doing a whole lot better than most."

"And that's the thing," said Dudley, pleased by the segue she offered him. "It would be better if he didn't have a day job. You know, so he can focus on painting."

"Oh, okay," said Amelia. "So you're thinking of sponsoring him?"

"Sort of," said Dudley. "I was thinking of becoming his patron."

"Right," said Amelia. "I guess that's what I meant. So what would a patron do for an artist in the twenty-first century? Supplement his income? Fund his shows? Or… what were you thinking?"

"Well," said Dudley, "what about the East Wing?"

Amelia didn't answer. She wiped her mouth with her napkin and gazed into the middle distance with a thoughtful expression. This was my cue to give them privacy. Collecting the coffeepot, I took my leave.

Even before the door was fully shut, I could hear Amelia forcing calm into the words: "The East Wing of *this house*?" and then I heard no more.

Mrs. Amelia Peterkin (née Hoffman) was the finest of women. She and Dudley fell in love in the final year of high school. Dudley had little to recommend himself to the attention of a smart, strikingly beautiful girl like Amy Hoffman, but she loved him regardless. Perhaps she was impressed by his genius with computers, or maybe she saw the purity of his young heart and had the wisdom to appreciate the scarcity of genuinely good men. The one certainty was that she did not fall in love with Dudley for his money, because when she accepted the engagement ring that he offered her on June 2, 2000, he didn't have a dime to his name.

An historian by profession, Amelia Hoffman was the author of eleven books, both popular and academic. From a strictly financial perspective, her successes could not be compared to those of her husband. In terms of professional status, however, she was a star in her own right, being renowned as one of the finest modern interpreters of Mediterranean history from AD 400–900. She traveled a good deal, often leaving for weeks at a time to conduct field research in the Balkans, North Africa, or the Iberian Peninsula.

My more cynical reader will be connecting unbecoming dots at this juncture. *Aha,* you might be thinking, *I know how this ends! Wealthy couple who issued promises of marital fidelity with no idea what their future would be? Long work trips that leave them apart and lonely for weeks on end? Rich as Croesus and stuck with a high school sweetheart? Let me guess!*

But my more cynical reader would be wrong. The love of the Peterkins was complete. They only understood romance in the context of their marriage and would never seek to discover it elsewhere. More than that, this love was so well understood between them that there could never be suspicion by one of the other. The world measured the immense wealth of Dudley against the elegant brilliance of Amelia, but that was not an exercise the happy couple ever engaged in. Both were firmly persuaded that they had gotten the better end of the deal in their youthful marriage and never sought to question the matter.

Mr. Patrick Hoffman, though, knew precisely who had gotten the better end of the deal.

"Morning, Lancaster!" he said as we passed in the hall.

"Good morning, sir," I replied.

"Are they already in there?" he asked.

"Yes sir."

"What are you doing with that coffee?"

"Just preparing a fresh pot, sir."

"Yes," he said approvingly. "That's absolutely right. It's just what I need."

I watched him make his slow way toward the breakfast room, his hands deep in his pockets. It was not my place to warn him that the air might be tense in that room, though I felt bad withholding this intelligence. Resigned to my limited sphere of influence, I continued toward the kitchen.

"Good morning, Dad!" Amelia greeted her father with her regular warmth, as if nothing at all was the matter.

Patrick Hoffman had served for much of his career in Her Majesty's Diplomatic Service. Travelling constantly and living in cities the world over had given him a rich storehouse of experiences. This lifestyle also accounted for Amelia's soft, unidentifiable accent and her excellent comportment, as she had spent most of her childhood at her father's side.

Hoffman was invited to join the Peterkin household as soon as they moved to Harper's Lane, which meant that he had been in that house for almost as long as I had. At first, I anticipated his arrival with some concern. He was very advanced in years and most, including his daughter, thought him a little senile. I once held a station in the city of Rabat where I was expected to serve as both butler and nurse to the household's declining member, and I was concerned that the Peterkins would have something similar in mind. I am not a nurse. I have all the respect in the world for nurses who facilitate the continuation of an intact household by contributing their care to a delicate situation, but I am a butler. I have neither the training nor the inclination to nurse.

Fortunately, Hoffman needed no such level of care. He was most definitely eccentric, but far from senile. His was the eccentricity of a man who has outgrown inhibition. What he loved, he loved; what he hated, he hated; what he didn't care about, he didn't care about. He squandered none of his dwindling store of energy disguising his feelings or putting on airs. It took me only a few days in his company to find that the mind of the man functioned very well indeed.

People often talk to household staff with the happy ease and liberty with which they address their therapists. In this, Hoffman was no exception. During those introductory weeks, he found me to be an agreeable companion. He would follow me sometimes as I conducted my evening inspection of the house and immediate grounds, gracing me with an endless stream of speech. Whether he was giving me his view of the day's events (always an enlightening perspective) or recounting an autobiographical anecdote from his years in the diplomatic service, he never ran out of thoughts to share.

This odd, somewhat lopsided friendship did not go unnoticed by my employers. A few weeks after Hoffman joined the household, I heard Dudley and Amelia discussing the matter within earshot of my desk. My office was along the same hall as theirs, and eavesdropping was a common practice among the three of us.

"Looks like Lancaster's made a friend," Dudley remarked.

"Do you think he minds?" Amelia asked.

"Doesn't seem to," said Dudley. "I'm certainly not going to say anything about it. I think it's good for your dad to have someone to talk to like that. Plus, it has him walking."

"They've started watching TV together," said Amelia.

"Really? Where?"

"In the library."

"The library. In the East Wing? Is there a TV in there?"

"Yep. I found them watching a terrible medical soap together and drinking schnapps. Most of the furniture is still sheeted, but they've uncovered two armchairs and have a little side table between them for the drinks."

"Watching a soap."

"Heckling it like Statler and Waldorf."

"Seems a little weird, doesn't it?"

"No," said Amelia with her pretty laugh. "It's cute."

*　　*　　*

(Wednesday, February 23)

Two days after Dudley Peterkin first introduced Amelia to the idea of the patronage, I was asked to join them in their sitting room. When I entered the study, I found that the Peterkins were already in the company of Hoffman. Dudley asked me to take a seat, and I complied, resisting the temptation to appear curious.

What followed, I'm sorry to say, was improper.

At first, Dudley and Amelia simply described the artist, Lucian Tremblay, and his work. Dudley expressed his interest in becoming the man's patron.

"Why does he need that?" Hoffman asked. "Is he trash?"

"No," said Dudley. "He's just not really discovered yet. I want to give him an opportunity to focus on his work so that he can get over his early career hurdles more easily."

"Sounds like he's trash," growled Hoffman.

"Dad..." chided Amelia gently.

Hoffman settled deeper into his armchair, sighing resignedly though his walrus mustache. It often fell to Amelia to prevent her father from giving Dudley a hard time. The old man had ceased bothering with diplomacy—or basic tact—when his long career came to an end. Retirement is retirement.

"The reason that we're bringing all of this to your attention," said Dudley, "is that we're considering offering use of the East Wing to Lucian Tremblay and his wife."

"On a trial basis," added Amelia quickly.

"Absolutely," said Dudley. "On a trial basis." It was clear that the necessity of a trial had been made very clear to him.

"But we're not going to make that invitation without talking to you two first," said Amelia. "You're as much members of this household as Dudley and me. If you don't like the idea, we won't do it."

"I don't like it," said Hoffman quickly.

Dudley muttered something under his breath.

"Okay, Dad," said Amelia, "let's think about it just a little bit more. This is quite important to Dudley. Lancaster, would you like to add anything?"

I smiled politely. "I appreciate your making me aware of potential changes to the household. It would be my pleasure to make all the arrangements required to ensure the comfort of your guests."

"Oh, we know," said Amelia. "We know that we can count on you to do a good job, Lancaster. That's not really the question. We want to know if you're comfortable with this whole idea. Like, personally."

I stiffened ever so slightly and felt my smiling lips pursing. My feelings about my employers' personal affairs did not seem pertinent. I appreciated the spirit of the gesture but would strongly have preferred that a boundary be maintained between my personal and professional relationship with the household. I was not merely a friend who lived with the Peterkins. I was their butler—an employee. Muddying the waters between the two inevitably led to complications in the professional relationship. I had seen it and even experienced it. Amelia should not have been asking me to approve her personal decisions.

"I'm sure that I can rely upon your judgement in this, as in all decisions like it," I said.

"We only ask because we know that you and Patrick enjoy using the library," said Dudley. "You'd have to move your TV time to some other room. Maybe your office?"

"Or even our living room!" said Amelia. "We don't mind watching TV with you two."

I could not have been stiffer. I straightened my glasses.

"That's true, Lancaster," said Hoffman. "We couldn't drink in there anymore. I don't like it."

"Lancaster?" said Amelia.

I took a deep breath. "It would be unthinkable—distressing, in fact—for me to contemplate you changing your plans on account of some small matter of my personal convenience.

If I may be so bold, I would request that you not consider my opinion any further in making your decision."

"Lancaster!" barked Hoffman. "Just say you don't like it! They'll only listen to you."

"Hey now," said Dudley lamely, "that's not true."

It was true, but there was nothing I could do about it.

A weekend invitation to Mr. and Mrs. Tremblay was dispatched by email that afternoon. It was accepted less than an hour later.

"Just a second, Lancaster," said Dudley.

I was standing by the door to the dining room, allowing the family to file in before beginning dinner service. Dudley was the last one to join the table, and it seemed that he had timed his arrival to allow for a brief, discreet conversation. To facilitate this further, I allowed the dining room door to ease shut while surrendering my full attention to my employer.

"Mr. Peterkin," I said.

"The Tremblays are joining us for a couple nights this weekend. If all goes well, we'll probably suggest the patronage to them before they leave."

"Very good, sir," I said agreeably.

"We'll put them up in the East Wing. That should help them decide."

"I will see to it that the rooms are all cleaned this week."

"Perfect. Thank you, Lancaster." Dudley nodded with firmness.

I gestured to the door. "May I?"

Dudley made no response at first and then, all in a rush, he blurted: "I'm sorry about this morning. That was tacky, wasn't it. I appreciate your professionalism, Lancaster. I respect it. I'm sorry if the way we did that kind of... I guess... offended you. I didn't think you'd like to be asked, but you know how Amy is. She hates not including you in the family council. She's got that much heart."

Dudley's eyes were focused on the upper panel of the door before him as he made this awkward little speech, but they darted toward me once he was done, searching for a reaction.

I nodded. "Thank you, sir." I could have said so much more, but sometimes simplicity is elegance.

Dudley smiled. "You're welcome," he said. "Thanks, Lancaster."

He and I said no more about it.

Amelia did, though. She joined me in the dining room as I was cleaning away the dinner things.

"Hi!" she said. She stood in the doorway, studying my face with her open, unaffected gaze.

"Mrs. Peterkin." I hope my tone was as cheerful as I felt. I always enjoyed time spent in her company.

"Sorry to bother you at your work," she said. She stepped in, her feet somehow making no sound at all.

"I'm far from bothered," I said.

"I was worried about you," said Amelia.

"Oh, I hope not," I said. "I am quite well." I looked up and met her gaze with a reassuring smile.

This was very like Amelia Peterkin. When Dudley said she had heart, he referred to how readily and deeply she cared about people. It was her greatest, most finely developed beauty, and she had many.

"I could tell that you were pretty uncomfortable this morning," said Amelia.

"I'm sorry to hear that," I said.

Amelia laughed lightly. "You can't hide it from me, Lancaster," she said. "I know you too well. You get so stiff and buttoned-up when you're uncomfortable."

"You have found my tell," I said good-humouredly.

"I spent too much of my childhood around diplomats," Amelia said with a wink. "I'm a mind reader now." She leaned against the credenza and brushed an invisible speck from her skirt with the back of her hand. My own mind-reading powers told me that her casual air was laying the groundwork for a casual question. "Lancaster," said Amelia, "I hope you didn't feel like we were railroading you in there."

"I beg your pardon?" I was stripping the table of its linen when she said this and paused.

"I just mean that you might have felt that Dudley and I were pressuring you into saying what we wanted to hear. I hope you would feel comfortable telling us if you don't like this patronage idea."

I resumed my stripping of the linen and found myself carefully folding the tablecloth, even though it was headed for the washing machine. Amelia noticed and drew in a long, sucking breath.

"Okay, okay," she said soberly. "It's fine, Lancaster. You don't have to say anything now. You'll get a chance to meet them this weekend. If that changes your mind, just come let me know."

I nodded and quickly balled up the linen. "I want to thank you," I said earnestly, "for showing such concern for my comfort, Mrs. Peterkin. I assure you that I find it quite touching."

"Of course, Lancaster," said Amelia. She pushed herself off the credenza, and in two light, silent steps she was at my side. She placed a hand on the sleeve of my coat and smiled at me. Her fingers' hold on the thick, woolen fabric was so ethereal that the coat wasn't so much as creased, yet with that hand on my arm I could no more move than if I had been shackled to a mountain. "You're a part of this family, Lancaster," she said sweetly. "We would be *ruined* without you. I know you're too proper to acknowledge this, but I'm not nearly so proper. You're one of us. Dudley and I are never going to take you for granted, I promise."

I forced a smile and looked down at the bundle of white cloth in my arms. It was not the first time that Amelia had said something similar to me. Time and time again she extended the olive branch of friendship. Each time she acknowledged my invaluability; each time she softly admonished me for being "too proper" to accept the gesture.

Each time, I was filled with sincere gratitude.

So it was. Dudley respected me. Amelia loved me.

My employers were the finest I had ever known.

Every ounce of love and respect that they felt for me was reciprocated. That was the truth that I had left unspoken in my conversation with Dudley; the truth that Amelia sought to confirm; the truth that filled my heart with every act of service that I performed in the execution of my duties.

* * *

It was that same love and respect that filled my heart when I asked the cleaners to work an extra two days that week so the East Wing would be ready. It filled my heart as I worked with Paige to plan the lunch menu for Friday. As I stood in front of the house on Friday morning, watching the Tremblays' car slowly make its way up the drive toward me, those same sentiments guided my thoughts. Perhaps, I told myself, this wouldn't be so bad. Perhaps having an artistic couple in the house would be interesting. If Dudley and Amelia were entertaining the idea, who was I to balk at it?

That winter had been unseasonably warm. As balmy weather made outdoor dining possible, and given that this was to be the Tremblays' first meal at Harper's Lane, the gazebo was the perfect place to lunch. A picture, we are told, is worth a thousand words, and the grounds of that property formed an excellent collage of the Peterkins' vision for the good life. Near the kitchen's back door was a small vegetable and herb garden. By the warden's cottage (where I lived) was a duckpond that we kept stocked with trout. There was a tennis court where Dudley and Amelia usually played before breakfast. There was a small orchard just east of the tennis court. Between and amongst all these features were lawns, flowerbeds, and a winding path of crushed seashells. The gazebo sat like a tall island in the centre of this paradise, connected to the house by an isthmus of stone that was itself flanked by old birches.

Paige had prepared a grilled veal cutlet laid in tender strips over a bright vegetable salad of slivered peppers, shredded green and yellow zucchini, and a little red onion. She and I had prepared a plate to taste earlier that day, and it was brilliant. The aesthetics of the dish were perfectly matched by their flavour profile. The veal was salty and just a little smoky. The salad of yellow, green, red, and purple was dressed with a sharp, citric vinaigrette that popped in the mouth almost as much as the vegetables popped on the plate.

I served an unchilled viognier with the meal, which I deemed a flawless pairing. Paige agreed.

Mrs. Tremblay did not.

Kandyss Tremblay was a woman whose appearance had a peculiar effect. Upon entering a room, she left people speechless; upon exiting, she left people with a good deal to talk about. Her hair was bleached, her lips were lifted, her nails were long, and she filled her clothes with little margin for error. Every aspect of her sensational appearance suggested a cartoonish parody of how one might overuse the beauty industry. Unfortunately, if there was any parody at work, Kandyss did not appear conscious of it.

As remarkable as was Kandyss's appearance, she made her most lasting impression when speaking. Her voice was reedy and incessantly plaintive. As she commented to Amelia on the beauty of the grounds, I was driven to distraction trying to decide whether she was deliberately talking like a child or if it was somehow a natural tone.

Kandyss didn't like the viognier.

She leaned back in her seat and cupped her hand around her mouth as if trying to be discreet. "Excuse me," she hissed at me in a sort of stage whisper. Quite naturally, it brought the conversation of the entire table to a halt.

I acknowledged her. "Ma'am?"

She held up her wine glass. "Is this like, the house wine?" she asked.

"It's not a restaurant, Kandy," muttered Lucian.

"That is the Cameron Manor Viognier," I said. "The grapes were grown not ten miles from here."

"It's got a funny taste," she said. To emphasise the word "funny" she wrinkled her nose.

"It's probably just nicer than what you're used to," said Lucian with an awkward snort of laughter.

"I'm *used* to chardonnay," Kandyss informed me confidentially.

"Please," I said, nodding understandingly. "Allow me to fetch you a chardonnay."

And I was gone. I took a shortcut through the kitchen door and found Paige spying through the window.

"What are they like?" she asked.

I made an effort to reserve judgement. "Mrs. Tremblay would prefer the chardonnay with her lunch," I said simply.

Paige whipped at me with a kitchen rag. "How does she seem?" she pressed.

"Not very adventurous when it comes to wine," I said. I passed down the kitchen steps into my cellar, winking at the cook as she issued a curse upon me for withholding my true impressions of the couple.

"It's not fair!" she cried from the top of the steps. "I do all the cooking and you get to see what kind of people they are! Don't hold out on me! It's not fair!"

"Let's just say I'm glad Mr. Hoffman decided to boycott this lunch," I said as I came back up the steps with a fat, gold-green bottle of chard. "I think he would find it even harder than usual to be civil."

I quietly poured the wine into a fresh glass for Kandyss, careful not to interrupt the flow of conversation.

"Can I have some ice?" Kandyss asked.

"Come on, Kan," muttered Lucian.

"Of course, ma'am," I said.

"Sorry," said Lucian to me, shaking his head.

I smiled. "I am in no way inconvenienced," I assured him.

"Could the ice be in a glass on the side?" Kandyss asked.

"Certainly."

"With a spoon?"

There was a heartbeat of silence from the other three as they all studied Kandyss wonderingly.

"Naturally," I said with a feudal nod.

"Well?" Paige greeted me as I burst into the kitchen once more.

I shook my head.

On my way back to the table, I saw Dudley eyeing me with an apologetic expression. I smiled reassuringly.

Lucian watched me set down Kandyss's ice and spoon with a grim smile. "Thanks, man," he said.

I glanced up from the table to make eye contact with the artist. His words were grateful, but his tone was apologetic. Maybe a couple years spent in the company of the blissful Peterkins had affected my expectations, but I was annoyed by Lucian's readiness to apologise for his wife. To my mind, it infantilised someone who didn't need any help in that department.

"It is my pleasure," I said stiffly.

Lucian detected my disapproval, and the corner of his mouth twitched in and out of a microscopic sneer. He turned away from me and gave Dudley a toothy grin. "Dudley. My guy. This is one hell of a backyard."

"Oh thanks," said Dudley. "I'm glad you like it. You know, when I was looking at that painting of yours—the one with no name?—I was kind of reminded of this."

"There are two halves to that painting," said Lucian, winking.

"Right!" Dudley laughed. "True. I don't mean the really depressing half. I'm talking about the green half with the trees and stuff. It's not a very exact comparison, just... I don't know... a vibe."

"Oh yeah," said Lucian. "Don't second guess yourself there, Dudley. I can see it too."

"What painting are we talking about?" asked Amelia.

"Hang on," said Lucian. He pulled out his phone and spent a couple minutes with his chin tucked against his chest, studying its screen and, presumably, searching through his photos for an image to show Amelia. "There it is," he said at last, handing the phone over to Amelia. "Your husband was completely captivated by this last Saturday."

Amelia took the phone and studied the screen with a slightly furrowed brow.

"It's probably not as impressive on a screen," said Dudley. "This was a huge canvas, Amy."

Amelia nodded.

Lucian turned back to Dudley. "Parties here must be wild."

"Not really our style," said Dudley. "This is our escape from craziness."

"No way!" Lucian looked about the grounds, adjusting his assessment of what he saw. He nodded. "I get it," he said.

Amelia handed Lucian back his phone. "Thanks," she said.

"No problem."

"Kandyss," said Amelia, "what do you do?"

Kandyss put down her glass. "I like this wine better," she said with a pucker. She grinned at me as she spoke, and I nodded my satisfaction. She turned back to Amelia. "But to answer your question, Amy... Oh, I don't know how to describe it... Lucy?"

"Kan?"

"How would you describe it?"

"Your work?"

"Yeah. How would you describe it?"

"Modelling."

"Oh wow!" said Amelia.

"No..." moaned Kandyss fanning herself with her fingers. "It's not just that. It's more of a promotional business. I'm self-employed. I work with a few different companies."

"Sounds great!" said Dudley.

"I love it," said Kandyss.

Lucian listened to this exchange impatiently. In the tiny lull following Kandyss's last remark, he leapt in. "Anyway!" he said. "Here's something I don't get. I've been doing more reading up on you, Dudley, and you've had a complete rockstar career. You're a genius and a billionaire and young and sexy. Then I was thinking about our conversation from last week. The one about your public image."

"Ah," said Dudley.

Amelia looked up, her expression bright with interest. She looked at Dudley questioningly, but he wasn't looking in her direction. Clearly, she hadn't heard any more about this conversation than I had.

Lucian continued. "It's hard to overstate the impact a guy like you would have if you decided to become a mover and shaker in the art world."

"I don't think I'm qualified to impact that world," said Dudley. "I wouldn't bring anything more than money to the table."

"I mean, at first, sure. But you'd get the swing of things. You have the instinct for it. I could be your guide until you found your feet."

"What are we talking about?" Amelia asked.

Lucian had an odd habit of closing his eyes when he needed to address someone new. He would close them, turn his head, and then reopen them once he was facing his new listener. He did so now, a very slight smile frozen on his face. It made him look like he was trying to be patient. "When we first met," he said to Amelia, "I tried to convince your husband that he should lean into his fascination with art. I said it would add something special to his public image."

"Dudley!" cried Amelia in mock horror. "You have a public image?"

Dudley grinned. "I will if Lucy here has his way."

Lucian seemed almost annoyed by this dismissive humour. "How can you stand to hide away in the middle of nowhere like this? Don't you miss the excitement of living in the middle of the action? Don't you miss the attention? Don't you miss being The Man?"

Dudley shook his head. "No?" He glanced at Amelia and then quickly looked back at Lucian. "Not really? Honestly, fame has always been kind of a burden to me. I've always had to put up with whatever notoriety comes with my work, but I way prefer being in a quiet home that I share with my best friend." He glanced at Amelia again, this time with a wink.

"Fine, fine!" Lucian spread his hands, surrendering to the consensus of his audience. "You're happy ignoring your public image as curated by tabloids. But that doesn't need to stop you becoming a prince in the world of art."

"If you say so," said Dudley.

Amelia was trying not to laugh. “Kandyss,” she said, changing the subject abruptly, “do you play tennis?”

“Yes,” said Kandyss.

“Sort of,” said Lucian.

“Do you play?” Dudley asked.

Lucian nodded. “Yep. Not well, but I try to get out there when I can.”

“Not more than me,” said Kandyss sulkily.

“That’s true,” said Lucian placatingly.

Amelia gave me a nod, and I started clearing the table.

After lunch, the Tremblays took a drive to explore the nearby hills and seashore. I heard the Peterkins enter the house, and their conversation in the front hall was clearly audible from where I was at work in the dining room.

“Wow,” said Amelia.

“They seem to like it here,” said Dudley.

“They were so…” said Amelia. I couldn’t see her, but I could imagine her looking around the room searchingly, as was her habit when words failed her.

“Kandyss seems like quite the character,” said Dudley.

“Kandyss? You mean Kandy? Kan? Kandy with the prepubescent larynx?”

I smiled as I tugged at the tablecloth, eliminating the last unwanted fold from its creamy surface.

“Amy! Don’t be mean.”

“I know. It’s whatever. But Dudley, don’t they seem like a funny pair? I mean, in terms of compatibility?”

"And in general."

"If it comes to that, we're kind of funny too," said Amelia.

"Speak for yourself," said Dudley.

There was a moment of hushed whispering and a giggle. I opened the silver drawer on the credenza with a deliberate bang, and the whispering ceased.

"Dudley," said Amelia, "I've been wanting to ask you—"

"Sorry," said Dudley. "I'm already married."

"Shut up. Tell me about this conversation you had with Lucy in New York."

"The one about public image?"

"I was surprised that you hadn't told me about it."

"There's not much to tell. It was basically just what he said. He thinks I should get into art. Become the billionaire art lover."

"What do you think about it?"

"I mean, it's kind of a fun idea."

"Really?"

"You know how much I like a good hobby, and the arts are important."

"Absolutely," said Amelia, "but is this really *your* hobby?"

"It could be."

"And what would it entail?"

"I don't know. That doesn't really matter right now. We still haven't answered the big question of the hour. What do you think of the Tremblays?"

Amelia sighed. "This is all a little weird, but I'm okay giving it a go if you're sure it's a good idea."

"Hey now," said Dudley. "You need to be sure too. It's a pretty big commitment for people we only just met."

"We could get the lawyers to write up a contract. NDAs and a trial period and terms and conditions. We could make sure it's not risky."

"It would mean having that woman in our house," said Dudley.

Amelia laughed. There had been a little tension in the air, and even I breathed a little easier when I heard that musical sound.

"And I'm okay with that, Dudley. Artistic couples are supposed to be eccentric. You said so yourself. Remember that it's not like they'll be in our space. They'll have their own wing with their own entrances and everything. We won't eat together, we won't hang out together, and we'll only see them if we want to. It'll be more like having neighbours than houseguests."

"Now I feel like you're trying to talk *me* into this," said Dudley. "I thought you'd be against it."

"I'm sure I could get on with them," said Amelia. "I can get on with anyone. Besides! They're colourful. As long as they're okay with the terms of the patronage, I'm game."

The terms were written up in a contract granting a trial period during which the Tremblays had access to the East Wing as well as a regular monthly allowance for personal expenses. In return, the Tremblays were to abide by a set of conditions. There were the more obvious terms that might be found in any tenant agreement, and then there were conditions that applied to the Peterkins' unique situation.

When I finally had an opportunity to read the agreement, I was pleased to see that "Use of Household Staff" commanded its own section. Any and all services or changes to services required by the Tremblays had to be made known to the chief-of-staff (myself) at least ninety-six hours in advance. This was a very constraining standard by which the Peterkins did not themselves abide, but I was glad to see it.

The patronage was proposed to the Tremblays on Saturday morning, and they accepted its terms later that day. The Tremblays were flying out Sunday morning, so Dudley asked me to sit down with them Saturday night to discuss their meal and cleaning schedules.

"We don't have to eat every meal with Dud and Amy, do we?" Lucian asked.

"No sir," I said. "Mr. Peterkin has made it quite clear that he wants you to be afforded as much privacy as possible. Your meals will be served in your own dining area unless other arrangements are made."

"Great."

"Meals are served at regular hours," I said. "Breakfast is at eight, luncheon at twelve-thirty, and supper at six-thirty. You will be attended by a servant who is moving in especially to care for you."

This was where Kandyss got involved. "That won't work," she said.

"Oh?"

"Eating breakfast at eight *every day?* Can't we just have breakfast, like, an hour after we get up? Unless we want breakfasts in bed! Lucy, what do you want? Let's keep it loose."

I straightened the pen beside my notebook so that it was perfectly parallel. We were seated in the library. It was the same library where Mr. Hoffman and I had enjoyed drinks and TV in the past. The screen of the television set over the fireplace stared blankly down at me like the phantom of a thing I had killed. I inhaled deeply.

"Perhaps," I said, offering my most deliberately servile smile, "I have done a poor job of explaining the situation. The Peterkins do not keep a service kitchen that turns out meals on demand. Instead, to avoid waste and promote a healthy routine, they employ a cook who carefully prepares meals that are served at set times."

"You're not—" Kandyss stopped herself and drew in a deep breath, as if sparing me from some sort of righteous wrath. "I don't think you see what I'm saying," she said in a very quiet voice. "What if I want to sleep in?"

I couldn't tell if Kandyss was more morally revolted by the idea of a routine breakfast time or by the idea of getting up at eight. Either way, I couldn't help but feel that neither of the Tremblays were trying as hard to be charming as they had when dining with my employers.

"If you wish to have an exception made to your regular breakfast time," I said, "I would be pleased to accommodate that. However, I would need to be made aware of the exception some time in advance."

"Okay," said Lucian, "how about this: We'll buzz you when we want breakfast served. That way you can just bring it whenever we want it. We don't always wake up at the same time. Sometimes we're early, obviously, but sometimes we're barely up before twelve. It's not worth it, you bringing breakfast when we won't be up for hours. Then you'd just have to make it again."

"I see," I said.

"Does that work?" Lucian asked.

"Not very well," I said. "However, I think I can suggest a compromise. What if I arrange to have a cold breakfast served for you at eight—something that won't spoil if you get up a little later. My underbutler will still ensure that you have hot coffee or tea whenever you wish to dine. If you particularly want a hot breakfast sometime, just let me know the day before, and I will make those arrangements for you."

"So, a continental," said Lucian.

"A continental?" Kandyss cocked her head to one side.

"Like at a motel," said her husband. His tone was bright and explanatory as if he were ignorant of the slight he directed toward me. I chose not to respond.

"Oh!" Kandyss beamed. "I like motel breakfasts!"

Lucian reset his jaw as he suppressed his frustration at his wife's reaction. He had hoped she would throw a fit over being served "motel food." Then he could apologise for her while continuing to push his own case.

Bastard.

I smiled politely because it is my duty to be agreeable to the Peterkins' guests, but also because I was pleased to see the artist fail in his attempt to weaponize his tacky wife. "I hope you will find it in every way superior to the continental breakfast served at any motel," I said.

When I told Paige what we were doing for the Tremblays' breakfasts, her eyebrows rose quickly.

"A cold breakfast," she repeated.

"It was a compromise," I said.

"So does this mean you're going to start making croissants and things?" she asked.

"Actually," I said, "I was hoping you would make the pastries for them."

She tilted her head forward as if looking over the rims of some imaginary spectacles at me. "Oh really," she said.

Paige Schopenhauer was a pretty woman. Though there was no great difference in our ages, she was still young enough to think me old without considering what that made her. A lifetime in kitchens had done nothing to round out her girlish frame, and this she attributed to her metabolism—her blessed metabolism, which I had heard about many times in the two years we had worked together. If ever I walked in on her eating in the kitchen, she would hastily wipe down the counter and make a remark about relying upon her metabolism. I don't know if she knew what the word really meant from a properly biological perspective, but I did know that when she referenced her metabolism, she meant two things by it: 1. "I can eat whatever I want without consequence." *and* 2. "Have you noticed how slim I am?"

Paige's hair was red where it wasn't grey, and her face was a dense mass of freckles and crow's feet. She never seemed to be outside, so I don't know how she came to be so freckled, but I didn't care. I liked her freckles. I liked her freckles, and I rather liked her red hair.

I also liked her eyes, and when she gave me that disapproving stare that she must have learned from some bespectacled librarian or other, I got to enjoy a long look into their pastel blue.

"Please?" I tilted my head, looking over my actual glasses at her.

"Sure," she said with a dramatic sigh, turning on her heel to walk away. "But only because I know you're dreading serving the croissants more than I'm dreading making them."

"I actually won't be serving them at all," I said.

"What?" Paige looked back over her shoulder at me. "Who's going to serve the artist?"

Liam Hendrix was a strapping, broad-shouldered young man who looked as though his entire life up until this moment had been spent in direct sunlight. His curly hair was a little bleached, and his skin bore a nutty tan. When I first met him, I will confess that his athletic appearance made me question his suitability. One so clearly given over to a physical lifestyle might well find it difficult to adapt to the delicate, domestic niceties of household work.

But young Liam was not a book to be judged by the cover. He had spent three years in hotels and was currently working at a private club that conducted a formal service à la russe in the dining room. He knew nothing about household management or service specifically, but when it came to food service, he was probably overqualified. His work in concierge was also of substantial value.

In an age when household domestics are a dying breed, recruitment often takes place from the ranks of high-end hospitality. It is not impossible to find graduates from true buttling colleges, but they are unlikely to have extensive experience while being very likely to want a full butler role. For an underbutler (little more than a glorified footman really, though that title sees little use these days) who would accept reasonable pay and have a teachable mind, I knew where to look.

Liam moved into Harper's Lane on March 30. He arrived in the afternoon with three tattered rucksacks, a bulging garment bag, and an Xbox. I showed him to the room that he would be occupying in the warden's cottage where I lived.

"This is a nice little place," said Liam, exploring the airy kitchen and living room where I led my own personal life.

"This cottage," I said, "like the house, is the personal property of Mr. and Mrs. Peterkin."

"Right," said Liam. He looked about him reverently. "I'll keep it tidy."

"Good man." I tried not to look too pleased, but I could not help cracking a small smile. I had been nervous about having to share the cottage, but Liam continued to impress me with his excellent domestic instincts.

"Do any other servants sleep here?" Liam asked.

"No," I said.

"Where does the chef sleep?"

"She does not reside on the property. She drives in from the town."

"Could I do that too?"

"Of course. But you'd have to pay rent in town. The Peterkins won't charge you for use of the cottage."

Liam seemed to be thinking. "Hmm..." he said. "What about the maids?"

"Our maid service is also brought in from town. Our employers are out of town often enough to justify an irregular cleaning schedule. The maids attend the house on Monday, Wednesday, and Friday. They do a very good job, and when they are absent, you and I will do our best to keep things up."

"So," said Liam. "Just you and me then. In the cottage."

"Yes." I began to run out of good reasons for this conversation. The only reasons left to consider were bad ones. "Is that all right with you, Mr. Hendrix?"

Liam blushed under his tan. "Yeah, for sure!" he said quickly. "I just..." He appeared to have completely lost his oars. He looked at the ceiling for a minute while he gathered his thoughts. "I have a girlfriend," he said.

There it was.

"Congratulations," I said.

"Just thought I'd mention it," said Liam somewhat lamely.

"Thank you."

"Do you have a girlfriend, Mr. Lancaster?"

"I do not."

"Have you ever had one?"

"Once. I was very young."

Liam nodded. "Okay! What happened with that?"

"I learned that girlfriends were not well suited to a man such as myself."

"Right." Liam stopped nodding.

"Because of the demands of the work."

"Oh, okay." The nodding resumed.

"I always feared that it would not be possible to be both an excellent butler *and* an excellent family man. And now..." I shrugged and gestured toward my face. "Now I'm old."

Liam seemed satisfied by this explanation. "That makes sense," he said happily.

"I'm glad you think so," I said, straightening my glasses. "Will you excuse me?"

And I went back up to the house.

After dinner, I was joined again by Liam.

"You're settled in?" I asked.

"Yes sir," he said.

There was a momentary awkward pause as I checked my watch. He clearly didn't want to resurrect our conversation from earlier but was also quite clearly a little embarrassed by it. I made no effort to relieve his discomfort.

"You were going to show me your evening routine," he prompted.

"Exactly," I said, placing my watch back in my waistcoat pocket. "We start indoors and work our way out. We want to start in areas the Peterkins are more likely to use after dinner and then clear out of them quickly. Then, as we work our way through the house, we're less likely to disturb their privacy. Lastly, I move outside to inspect the grounds before locking the exterior doors and retiring to the cottage. At that point, the Peterkins have the house to themselves."

"Makes sense," said Liam.

And we began. It being a Wednesday, there was nothing to note in our inspection of the house. The maids had been in that day, and the common rooms were immaculate.

The awkwardness with which this tour had begun was quickly dissipated by the efficient diplomacy of cooperative work. As we made our way through the house, ensuring that everything was orderly and tidy, I lectured at length on the household standards which I strove to maintain. I felt that Liam was listening carefully, and this happy suspicion was confirmed by his frequently plying me with insightful questions.

We moved outside to begin our inspection of the immediate grounds, where we were greeted by Hoffman. He was easily a hundred yards off, but it didn't stop him addressing me.

"Lancaster!" he shouted.

"Good evening, Mr. Hoffman!" I returned. To Liam I quickly murmured, "Mr. Patrick Hoffman—Mrs. Peterkin's father."

"Ah," said Liam.

Hoffman drew near. He assessed Liam with a jaundiced eye. He had not yet met the young man, having been absent when the Peterkins did their customary introductory interview. In fact, for the past few weeks, Hoffman had been hard to find. He had avoided me generally about the house, and without either of us saying anything about it, we had stopped meeting in the library for drinks. He was mad at me for not opposing the patronage. There was no proper way for me to apologise without seeming to disrespect the wishes of my employers. So instead, I simply stood by and waited for Hoffman to decide that he had shunned me long enough.

"Mr. Hoffman," I said, "may I introduce Mr. Hendrix? He will be joining the household as my underbutler, specially to serve the East Wing."

"Ha!" grunted Hoffman. He looked away from Liam, apparently done with him. "So this is happening."

"Do you refer to the patronage of Mr. Tremblay?" I hazarded without hazard. "Yes sir. They are moving in on Monday."

Hoffman swore savagely.

Liam didn't so much as blink at the expletive. His face was utterly impassive, betraying neither amusement nor disapprobation. I was pleased. His experience was showing.

"I trust you are well this evening, Mr. Hoffman?" I said, changing the subject.

"Would be," he said. He paused and then started over. "Would be under different circumstances." For some people this vagueness of expression would be a sign of discretion, but for Mr. Hoffman it was simply a sign that he was trying to collect his fast-scattering thoughts. "Don't much care for this kid." He gestured at Liam.

"I am sorry to hear it," I said.

"Too tan," he growled. "He should be working in a surf shop."

Liam offered a small, inoffensive smile, inviting the possibility that this was an expression of the old man's humour. It was not, but the lad was right to try.

"Mr. Hendrix comes with an excellent resumé," I said. "He possesses extensive service experience."

"At least he's wearing a bloody coat," said Hoffman with a begrudging nod. "The other boy was just running around in a T-shirt like he owned the place."

I cocked my head. "The other boy?"

Hoffman turned and gestured behind him toward the corner of the house. "Over there. Saw him slouching around with his phone out. How many new staff have you hired, Lancaster? There's only two of these Tremblays, aren't there? Don't exactly need a whole regiment to watch over them."

"Mr. Hendrix is the only one," I said. "Mr. Hoffman, if you would excuse me, I would like to go find this young man you saw. Around the west end of the house?"

"Just there," said Hoffman, pointing again. "Can't miss him."

"Come on," I said to Liam.

We found him easily. A slim-limbed young man stood under one of the study windows, using his phone as a periscope to look inside.

I swallowed, and utilising as deep a voice as I could muster, bellowed: "Hey! You there!"

He was off like a whippet, his phone still in his hand, his chin tucked against his chest. I started after him, regretting instantly that I had not used stealth to shorten the distance before alerting my prey. I was not as fast as I had been in my younger days, and my lungs began petitioning me for a reprieve after only a few paces.

A sound like that of a galloping Clydesdale came thundering up behind me. In a flash, the substantial figure of Liam Hendrix shot by, covering ground like an Olympic sprinter. His gait was rapid and his stride long. As I staggered to a coughing halt, my hands grasping my knees, I continued to watch in amazement as my new underbutler tore across the smooth lawns of the Peterkin estate after his quarry.

"Runs like a bloody animal!" Hoffman observed.

I straightened quickly, attempting to regain the dignity that my attempt at running had cost me. "Mr. Hoffman," I said breathlessly, "perhaps you ought to go indoors until Mr. Hendrix and I have had a chance to sort this out."

"Shut up, Lancaster," said Hoffman cheerfully.

I was more than happy to oblige, as I had not yet fully caught my breath.

"Runs with his shoulders," said Hoffman approvingly. "That's what it is. Good form."

I didn't know what he meant by this statement but doubted that Hoffman had any idea what good form looked like in a sprinter. It occurred to me, as I panted and Hoffman chatted away, that this incident would likely heal the rift between us.

"Stop! Let me go, man! I'll just leave. I'll leave, okay? Just let me leave. Won't come back. Why the—let go!"

I turned at this tirade to observe Liam marching the trespasser toward us, his arm twisted behind his back. Expletives and obscenities flowed from the spidery youth like a stream of poison. His unkind descriptions of his captor did nothing to affect Liam's disposition. The underbutler was beaming like a dog enjoying a good game of fetch.

"Nicely done, Jimmy," said Hoffman.

I closed the distance between myself and the two young men, hoping that Hoffman would let me deal with this alone. "Explain yourself!" I barked.

"I just wanted to take pictures!" whined the intruder. "I've never seen a house like this before!" He sneered at me. "Must be nice, being rich! Hey? What, you're going to punish me for window-shopping your privilege? Screw you, old man!"

I refrained from engaging with the particulars of his tirade. "You're a thief," I informed him. "If you're not, then explain why you're skulking about taking pictures of the inside of my employer's residence?"

"Oh! This is your boss's place? Man. Must be tough!" Learning that I was not the owner of the estate had done nothing to dull his contempt.

I removed my phone from my inner jacket pocket. "I'm calling the police," I said.

"No. No! No?" He tried out a few different intonations before settling on begging. "Please? I was just curious! Couldn't help myself. I saw pics of this place on Insta and thought I'd check it out. I honestly wasn't going to steal anything."

"On Instagram?" I hesitated, my thumb hovering over the number pad on my phone. I glanced over my shoulder and saw that Hoffman had drawn near and was watching with an excited expression. I turned back to the rascal. "It would not be like my employers to reveal their place of residence on social media."

"I don't know what to tell you," he said. "Your employer named Kandy Kane?"

"Kandy," I repeated. "With a K?"

"Yeah," he said. "That's the hottie. Lucky you! Dang! What I'd give for your job."

"She was a guest here," I said. "This is not her property."

"Shut up!" He took a moment to describe Kandyss Tremblay in ungentlemanly terms. "Let me..." He wriggled, and Liam tightened his grip. "Come on! Let me get my phone out! I'll show you!"

I nodded to Liam, and the underbutler loosened his hold.

"There!" The thief opened his phone, and after a moment of thumbing through posts, held it up for my inspection.

There indeed. He was showing me a picture of Kandyss Tremblay posing all over the fountain in the center of the driveway's roundabout. Behind her towered the Peterkin home. Underneath this gaudy photograph was the caption "Home sweet home! #thatnewhomesmell" and several other hashtags that aren't worth listing. The location was pinned on the post.

"Lancaster," said Hoffman. I turned and gave him my attention. He was smiling and holding forth his own cell phone. "Take his picture," he said. "Take his picture and text me with his phone. If anything goes missing, we'll give his picture and number to the police. Simple as that."

"Yeah!" said the young would-be burglar. "Do what the old man says! He's your boss! You have to, right?"

I stared at Hoffman for a steady moment, trying to read his intentions.

"Do it," said Hoffman.

"Very good, sir," I said.

The deed was easily done. The thief smirked and jeered while I photographed him and made no protest when I used his phone to send Hoffman a text. No doubt he considered it preferable to being interviewed by the police. I wondered if they would have recognised him.

"Let him go," I said to Liam. "Here," I passed the phone back to the thief. "Get off this property immediately."

The thief sneered at me in return and pushed past. "Thanks, Old Timer," he said to Hoffman.

Hoffman's hand shot out and grabbed the thief's upper arm. I could tell by how the boy winced that Hoffman's grip was strong. "I won't forget this," said Hoffman in a low, sinister voice.

"Great! Fine! Whatever, dude! Let me go! Frick! I should call the police on *you guys!* That's a lot of manhandling!"

We followed the thief around the side of the house and watched him until he had passed through the gates at the foot of the drive and was gone.

(Thursday, March 31)

"Hi Kandyss," said Amelia.

I was in my office, which was across from Amelia's on the second floor of the West Wing. Both our doors were open, as was our custom. Dudley's was next to Amelia's, and we often left our doors open, occasionally engaging in near-shouted conversations across the hall.

Paige and I were finalising a shopping list for her to take into town that afternoon. Amelia was on the phone.

"Should I shut the door?" Paige whispered.

I pretended not to have heard her, staring at her grocery list without reading it. Hoffman had related the events of the night before to the

Peterkins over breakfast that morning, and Amelia had assured Dudley that she would handle the necessary conversation with Kandyss.

"We're really looking forward to Monday as well, Kandyss," said Amelia. "There's just a quick conversation you and I need to have about security." There was a pause. "Yes. Well, it's a little thing, but actually pretty important. You posted pictures of our home on social media with the location included. Yeah. Yes. I don't know. I only saw the Instagram post. Where else did you post it? Oh! Okay..."

But Paige got up and shut the door at that point.

"Thank you," I said.

"Oh sure," said Paige. "Like you were just about to go shut it yourself."

(Monday, April 4)

By the time the Tremblays arrived the next week, Mrs. Tremblay (aka Kandy Kane, apparently) had learned that she was not to share any particulars about the house or its location on social media. The first thing that Lucian did upon stepping out of their car was apologise at length for the inconvenience that her indiscretion had caused. He was far too liberally forgiven by Mr. Peterkin.

"It was nothing," said Dudley. "I'm sure it won't come up again."

I should have liked to share his confidence.

"Dudley's an idiot," said Hoffman.

I made no response. I watched as the setting sun's rays brightened the tawny port in my glass.

I swirled the crystal and watched the brown and plum hues folding in and over each other. I heard Hoffman grab the bottle that sat on the ledge between us. Its hard glass rasped on the stone as he pulled it toward himself. The stopper came out with a sucking pop, and there was a splash as he refilled his glass. I glanced toward him to ensure he had replaced the stopper.

"More?" Hoffman was still holding the bottle.

I shook my head, holding up my glass to show him that it still boasted a couple ounces to its name.

"You heard me," he said, picking up the stopper and pushing it back in with a squeak of cork against glass. "He's a bloody idiot."

"I'm sure I wouldn't say anything of the kind," I said with some feeling. "Mr. Peterkin is a good and generous man. More than that, he is my employer. His deficiencies are not mine to discuss."

"Well, how about this *artist?*"

I said nothing, looking back down at my glass.

"You going to drink that?" Hoffman goaded me. "If you wanted it to age, you shouldn't have opened the bottle."

I smiled and took a sip. Warm. Full. Sweet. I was pleased. I turned around and slouched against the ledge. I looked at the house, so stately and handsome. My eyes wandered over the gothic, windowed gables that gave such light and dimension to the offices of the West Wing. Then my eyes made their way down to the East Wing. I felt my smile twist and fall. I took another, larger sip of port, this time with less pleasure.

Hoffman was watching me gravely as he leaned forward over the rail of the gazebo. “They won’t last long,” he said. “It simply won’t work out.”

(Friday, April 8)

As the week progressed, it appeared that Hoffman had been incorrect. The Tremblays had settled in quietly and without further incident. In fact, during most of the day it was possible to forget that they lived at Harper’s Lane at all.

“Why are you bringing the coffee?” Lucian asked when I entered the East Wing. He didn’t look displeased but was surprised that I wasn’t Liam. “Is the kid okay?”

“Mr. Hendrix is quite well,” I said with a small smile. I hoped the smile would be both friendly and reassuring. I know Paige would have said it was creepy. I can’t be everything to all people.

Lucian looked a bit uncertain. “Oh good,” he said. “Glad to hear it. Is it his day off?”

“Not at all,” I assured him. “I am serving you this morning in the hopes of checking in on you and Mrs. Tremblay. I would like to be sure that you are being well and thoroughly cared for.”

“Great. Yeah. Go ahead and do your thing.”

“Is that our boy?” sang Kandyss from somewhere above our heads.

“It’s Lancaster,” called Lucian unenthusiastically. He sat on the dining room table and accepted a cup of coffee from me.

“Oh! Lancaster!” said Kandyss, pronouncing the *s* as *sh.* “One second, I’ll be right down.”

The East Wing had been built expressly for hosting longer-term guests. The upstairs sported four substantial bedrooms (each with a gable that mirrored the gables on the West Wing). Significant renovations had transformed the downstairs into a sprawling living space with a modern, open-concept aesthetic.

The dining table on which Lucian was sitting was a single, gigantic piece of live-edge mahogany that had been entirely covered in a very thick coat of chip-proof polyester resin so that it was perfectly, flawlessly white. I considered it gaudy. Mr. Peterkin had deemed it creative and elegant. Lucian seemed to have confused it for a chair.

While I appreciated my employer's pursuit of the impressive and the elegant, I considered the room in which the horrible white table sat to be a better example of both. Rising above the table was a two-storey, vaulted ceiling. Banistered halls surrounded the open space, allowing communication from the bedrooms to the flight of stairs that descended west of the dining area.

"How have you found your first week?" I asked.

"Fine!" Lucian nodded. He sipped his coffee. "We like Liam. Good kid. Easygoing."

"I am very pleased to hear it. And you'll let him know if we can make any slight adjustments to your menus or service?"

"We can let him know? Not you?"

"Whatever you find most convenient, sir. Liam will bring any requests to me, naturally."

"Everything's been great."

"Perfect."

"Well. Except..." Lucian blew thoughtfully on his coffee.

"Sir?"

"Tell me about your mistress."

I blinked. "Are you referring to Mrs. Peterkin?"

"You don't call her that?"

"I do not."

"Tell me about her."

"Mrs. Peterkin is my employer," I said firmly, "and an excellent one at that. It would be both inappropriate and painful for me to engage in gossip at her expense."

"Oh no!" Lucian looked shocked. "Gossip? Nothing like that."

"I'm sorry if I spoke out of turn," I said. Perhaps I had been hasty. "Why don't you be more specific?"

"I'm just wondering if she's a snob."

"Sir!"

"No, no, Lancaster. That's not gossip. I'm just trying to figure out how to get on with your employers. I wouldn't want to offend them. You wouldn't want that either."

"Perhaps that's a matter for you to discuss with Mrs. Peterkin directly."

"Don't be an ass. I can't ask *her* if she's a snob. It's just that since the first time I met her, we haven't really... vibed. You know what I mean? Dud and I vibe. Liam and I vibe. You and I vibe. Right?"

"I am gratified to hear you say so, sir."

"But Amy? You'd think that she was actual freaking royalty. She doesn't think I'm funny. But! She does think it's funny that I'm trying to get Dud into art. You know I asked her to play tennis with me yesterday? A friendly gesture, right? Well, she said she normally only plays before breakfast during the week. The hell kind of excuse is that?"

"Will you require anything further for your breakfast, Mr. Tremblay?"

"That's it? You've got nothing?"

"I'm afraid—"

"Is it Kan?"

"I beg your pardon?"

"I feel like Kan is kind of a lot sometimes. Maybe your mis—employer doesn't take me seriously because she only sees me with Kandyss. Probably just writes me off. Like, it's as if nobody who married Kan could be capable of—" He stopped suddenly.

I heard the footsteps of Kandyss sounding above me again. She was leaving her room and circling the empty space above the dining area. I glanced at Lucian and saw that he was watching his wife's approach. Without thinking, I instinctively followed his gaze and instantly regretted the wandering of my eyes. I returned my attention to the French press, but not before Lucian noticed the turning of my head.

"Don't tell anyone what we've been talking about."

"I hardly think that *we* have been talking about anything," I returned, struggling to keep a professional friendliness in my voice.

"You can just leave that there," he snapped. "I'll pour Kan's coffee myself."

"Is there anything else I can get for you and Mrs. Tremblay before I go?" I asked in an amicable tone. I had worked in service long enough to know that Lucian's sourness was best ignored. One doesn't want to encourage a pouty streak.

"We're fine," growled Lucian.

"Very well," I said.

"Lancaster!" Kandyss was approaching us wearing a bright pink onesie.

"He was just leaving," said Lucian.

I was not quite out of the East Wing when Lucian started talking about me. Only a moment was needed before the connecting door between their wing and the main hall would finish swinging shut and the Tremblays and I would be permitted our mutual privacy. Lucian didn't wait for that moment to pass.

"What a snotty old queen," he said loudly.

I shut the door with immaculate care. I even turned the handle before pressing the door into its frame so that there was no clicking. I stood very still for a moment. I wasn't eavesdropping. I was straightening my cuffs. They had ridden a little high while I was pouring Lucian's coffee. I focused on the sound of the wool brushing the cotton of my shirt sleeve as I adjusted and readjusted my coat. I could feel myself becoming calm as I balanced the amount of shirt cuff visible. I straightened my waistcoat and tugged gently but firmly at my lapels to make sure the jacket was sitting forward against my collar.

"Hi there," said Paige as I entered the kitchen. She had just arrived herself and was sitting on the kitchen counter grinning at me like the cat that ate the canary. The source of her impudent pride, Liam, was standing beside her eating a pastry. She had spent the last week in heaven, pleased to no end at having Liam in the household. Hers was the shameless flirtation of a woman whose object of admiration was unattainable enough that her attentions could be considered harmless.

"Good morning, Miss Schopenhauer," I said politely.

Paige's grin slacked. She slid off the counter. "What's up?" she asked.

"Nothing at all," I said. I smiled.

She frowned. "Don't go coming in here with that grim face and your proper 'good mornings,' and expect me to just ignore it. Liam, why don't you give us a moment?"

Liam nodded, quickly scarfing down the last of the pastry and moving toward the door with his jacket over his arm.

"No!" I said quickly, then realised I had said it a bit loudly. I shook my head and laughed. "No, no! There's no need. Don't let me interrupt you two. I was just in the East Wing."

"Ah," said Paige. "Lucky you."

"If you say so," I said. I was still feeling a bit stiff. "Mr. Hendrix, you are aware that it would not be appropriate to gossip about the Peterkins with the Tremblays, correct?"

"I wouldn't do that," said Liam quickly. "Did they say I did that?"

"No." I shook my head. "No. It's fine. I just wanted to make sure you knew how inappropriate that would be." I tried to lighten the mood. "Speaking of inappropriate," I said, "does Mrs. Tremblay always dress like that in the mornings?"

"How was she dressed?" Paige asked before Liam could respond.

"Like a child," I said.

Paige grimaced and drew back her head as if I had broken a rotten egg. "What is the deal with that woman?" she asked with some heat. "What kind of weird world does she think she lives in?"

"What happened to not gossiping?" Liam asked.

"We're in the kitchen," said Paige. "This is where we talk about things. Those are the rules."

"Oh okay," said Liam, licking custard cream from his fingers, "I didn't know that Mr. Lancaster's rules didn't apply in here."

"Don't take that too far," I said.

"We're talking about Kandyss," said Paige.

"Right," said Liam. "I think she acts like that because she's an influencer."

Paige and I exchanged glances. Neither of us was about to admit in front of the other that this comment left us somewhat in the dark. Fortunately for us, Liam was happy to supply more details.

"She has promotional accounts for health and beauty products. She also poses as a fitness inspiration of sorts."

The old people sought to understand, and to that end, Liam gave a quick tour of Kandyss Tremblay's Instagram.

"Why is she always dressed like this on her social media?" Paige asked.

"Perhaps she's devoted to swimming," I suggested.

Paige looked at me with an expression that seemed to accuse me of something unseemly. I cocked my head questioningly, and she responded by pinching my arm. I blushed. I wasn't sure why she was teasing me, but I wasn't going to complain.

Liam seemed to have missed everything that had passed between Paige and me in that moment and sought to answer her question. "She promotes cosmetic and bath products," he said. "Shampoos and lotions and stuff. Sometimes clothing."

"Do you mean she makes money off this nonsense?" Paige asked.

"She definitely makes something," said Liam. "She has almost a hundred thousand followers."

"How does the money work?" I asked, genuinely mystified. "Who's paying her?"

"Obviously," said Paige, "it must be the companies that sell the hair products and things that pay her."

"I hope I'm not interrupting anything," said Mrs. Peterkin.

We three jumped, and Liam pressed the power button on his phone, deftly secreting away the object of our fascination. We turned en masse, all of us speaking at once to reassure the lady of the house that she posed no interruption.

Amy smiled at the guilty trio before her, and her eyes came to rest on me. I was keenly aware of a warm, tingling blush that was swelling in the soft of my cheeks. "Lancaster," she said, "are you available just now?"

"There are two things," said Dudley as soon as I stood before him in the Peterkins' living room. "The first has to do with the Tremblays."

"Well," said Amelia.

"Well?"

"Well *both*... really..."

"Well, that's true," said Dudley. "Both things have to do with the Tremblays. I guess I was just thinking that the second thing had more to do with Liam."

"Well, I guess you're right," said Amelia.

I waited for the exchange to conclude. It is difficult to convey how endearing all such interactions between the Peterkins were. One could read the way they corrected one another and overused the word "well" and think they must have been on the verge of a domestic. Such was not the case. If one could have watched their smiles and sparkling eyes as they spoke; if one could have heard the respect and care that warmed their every word; if one could have been there, one would have been watching them with the same expression of contented admiration that I wore.

"The Tremblays have a dog," said Dudley.

I started slightly, partly because I had not realised that the conversation had moved on to an actual agenda item and partly because that item was itself unexpected.

"They *have* a dog?" I repeated. "I assume that it is not yet on the premises?"

"Apparently, it's at his sister's place. They weren't going to mention it until they'd been here for a few days."

I made no comment, but not because I had none to offer.

Amelia spoke up. "They say it's not a big dog, and that it's very well house-trained. Can we leave you to figure out what needs to be done to get ready for its arrival?"

I nodded. "Naturally. When are they hoping to move the animal in?"

"Next weekend," said Dudley. "His sister will be bringing the dog Friday evening and staying over until Sunday morning. Actually, I forgot to mention that. Sorry, Lancaster. Short notice, I know."

"That's no trouble at all," I said. It really wasn't.

"We didn't know ourselves until last night," said Amelia. I could tell by a certain *je ne sais quoi* in her voice that she was no more impressed by this surprise than I was.

"The second thing," said Dudley, moving on, "is Liam."

"Yes?"

"How's he working out?"

"Extremely well, so far."

"Oh good," said Amelia. "That's what we thought too. Adding a dog to the East Wing will probably involve extra duties for him."

"Naturally."

"And that'll be okay?"

"Yes ma'am."

"They do keep saying that he's really well trained," said Dudley.

Amelia punched his shoulder. "Just like you."

Dudley narrowed his eyes in mock exasperation. "What do I have to do to get a little respect around here?" he asked me.

I gave a small but sincere chuckle. I was both charmed and amused. After my interaction with the Tremblays that morning, spending time with the Peterkins was like therapy.

(Monday, April 11)

"Hi Lancaster."

I sat back from my computer and made to rise.

Dudley waved me back into my seat. "No, no, no," he said. "You're good. Just wanted to see how you... what you were up to."

"I'm just updating my expenses sheet," I said.

"Right. Sorry." Dudley exhaled loudly. He seemed disoriented.

"Not at all, sir. This is a duty that makes me welcome any interruption."

"Good stuff. Great. Liam is still doing well?"

"Yes sir." I wondered what the purpose of this conversation could possibly be. Something was on my employer's mind but, uncharacteristically, he seemed reluctant to speak.

"Dudley?" Amelia had seen her husband standing in my office and removed her headphones.

"Amy!"

"You bugging Lancaster?"

"I am." Dudley gave me a last apologetic look and moved across the hall to his wife's office. "I can bug you, if you'd prefer."

"I booked the flight for Lucy's sister. I invited her to stay for a few days if she'd like."

"Oh! Okay!" Dudley sounded nervous. "I'm glad you mentioned that. I was talking to Lucy yesterday, and he wants to go to New York this week. He'll help his sister get the dog's stuff together and fly back with her."

"Oh!" Amelia turned back to her computer screen. "They'll want to be on the same flight headed back then. Has he booked yet?"

"I don't think so."

"I'll make it two seats then."

"Might want to make it three."

"The dog doesn't need a seat, Dudley. I think they have a special compartment for animals."

"Ha! Right. I know. It's just that I'll probably be going with Lucy."

Amelia looked up at him. "Oh okay," she said. "Why?"

"It's whatever. He wants to introduce me to the art scene where he started out. I guess there's a bunch of art galleries and stuff he wants to show me. He says it's vital for me as his patron."

"I get that," said Amelia, nodding slowly. She was gazing thoughtfully at her husband. "Do you have time for this, Dudley?"

"Oh yeah," said Dudley airily. "I'll make time."

"May I come?"

"Of course! I was hoping you could."

"I can't." Amelia said with a wink and a smile.

"Amy!" Dudley sounded genuinely disappointed.

"Unlike you," said Amy, "I have no magical powers. I can't just make time."

Dudley sank into a chair next to his wife with a sigh. "So," he said, "I have to visit these galleries with only Lucy to hide behind?"

"You'll survive," said Amelia. "When are you boys flying out?"

"Tomorrow."

Dudley and Lucian flew out first thing Tuesday, and the succeeding couple of days were remarkably quiet. Both Amelia and Kandyss seemed to have their own respective work to focus on, leaving the household staff entirely alone. That is, until Thursday evening after dinner.

I didn't know anything was amiss until I walked in on Amelia and Paige talking in the kitchen. That in itself was not alarming. Paige had none of my professional inhibitions about forming personal relationships with her employers, and she had long entertained a friendship with Amelia.

I was more concerned when I saw Amelia's expression. She was sitting on the counter and glanced toward the door as I entered. Her mouth wore a tight frown, and her knotted brows gave her a world-weary look. She slipped off the counter hurriedly when she saw me.

"I beg your pardon," I said. "I can come back."

Amelia forced a smile. "I was just leaving," she said.

"No, you weren't!" cried Paige.

"It's no trouble," I said. I began backing away.

Paige crossed the kitchen in my direction. I briefly wondered if I could outrun her. She took my arm. "Mr. Lancaster," she said. "We could use a man's perspective."

"If I come across a man," I said stiffly, "I shall send him to you at once." Despite my protests, I allowed Paige to lead me over to the counter where she and Amelia had been sitting.

"Lancaster won't want me to talk about this with him," said Amelia. "It's too personal."

"Mr. Lancaster is wise," said Paige. "It comes with his age."

"I would not want to be drawn into a discussion of personal or delicate matters," I said. "Mrs. Peterkin is quite right."

"Shut up," said Paige brightly. "Go ahead, Amy."

Amelia glanced hesitantly between Paige and me. "I don't think Lancaster wants to be part of this conversation."

"Yes, he does," said Paige. "He's just too shy to ask for an invitation."

"Well," said Amelia. "I did try, Lancaster."

"Consider me grateful, ma'am."

"Paige and I were just talking about Dudley's relationship with Lucy Tremblay."

I tugged at my left lapel.

"Stop that," said Paige, slapping my hand.

"Paige," said Amelia, "let him go."

"I'm sorry that I can't be of more use to you," I said. The apology was more than a formality. I made for the door and turned. "Mrs. Peterkin," I said, "though I must decline the privilege of this conversation, I hope that you will not think me indifferent to your happiness."

"It's okay," said Amelia softly. "Have a good night, Lancaster."

I received a text from Paige about thirty minutes later: *Coast clear.*

I returned to the kitchen and found Paige making two mugs of tea. She greeted me with a smile. "Welcome back," she said.

"Is everything all right, Miss Schopenhauer?"

"Nope," said Paige, passing me my tea.

"I am sorry to hear it. Mrs. Peterkin looked perturbed."

"She was. You should have been more sympathetic."

"We serve best," I said, "when we serve within boundaries."

"Maybe you do."

"I like to think so."

Paige blew on her tea and watched me expectantly.

I blew on my own tea.

"Well?" Paige prompted. "Aren't you going to ask what we were talking about?"

"I wouldn't want to be found prying," I said.

"So you're just here for the tea."

"And your company, Miss Schopenhauer."

Paige snorted. "Fine. I'll be the indelicate one, Mr. Lancaster, but you force my hand." She set her mug on the counter and hopped up next to it.

With some effort, I joined her. "Here." I produced a sleeve of jammy dodgers from my pocket. "I brought these."

Paige pinched my arm and took a cookie. "Amy's worried that Lucy is getting to Dudley."

"Getting to him?" I also took a cookie.

"Being a bad influence."

"Mr. Peterkin is hardly a child."

Paige looked at me with suspicion. "Are you taking his side?"

"Certainly not. It wouldn't be my place to take anyone's side. I just meant that I would have thought Mr. Peterkin old and wise enough to resist the influence of a wayward friend. That seems like a concern we might have if he were a teenager."

"Amy thinks he's having a midlife crisis."

"And why is that?"

"Do you know where he is right now?"

"Acquainting himself with some segment of the art scene in New York City," I said. "That and fetching a dog."

Paige produced her phone. "Look."

I looked, and my eyebrows rose. Paige was showing me a photo of Dudley Peterkin standing in a gallery, his chin resting in his hand, a thoughtful expression on his face. His hair was tousled, and he was wearing a loud, patterned shirt I had never seen before.

"What is this?" I asked.

"Lucy posted this on social media."

"I see."

"There's more too. Amy says he was supposed to be going to an event this week. Something to do with the teacher charity. He blew it off to go with Lucy."

"Perhaps we shouldn't question his judgement too freely," I suggested.

"It was an important event," said Paige insistently. "There were teachers there who signed up to serve with his organisation. He was supposed to give a speech."

I bit my cookie and chewed slowly before washing it down with tea. "Miss Schopenhauer?"

"Mr. Lancaster?"

"We must continue to have faith in the united character of our employers. Even if there has been a small course deviation, I am confident that, working together, they will correct themselves."

"Sure," said Paige. "Just as soon as Amy gets her hands on Dudley."

(Friday, April 15)

"Are you good with dogs?" I asked Liam.

"Normally, yes," said Liam uncertainly.

"This doesn't look like a normal dog," said Paige.

"How about you?" I asked her. "Are you good with dogs?"

"I love dogs," said Paige, "but I'm not sure what I think of this thing."

"He seems a bit off," agreed Liam.

"He's ugly as sin," said Paige.

She wasn't wrong. Cartoons would lead one to think that an animal with a big head and huge eyes would be cute. This was not true of

Hieronymus. He was a mixed-breed animal uniting the lineages of Jack Russell terriers and Italian greyhounds. I don't know if all animals of that particular genetic recipe are staggeringly unattractive, or if Hieronymus was just a special case. His bug-like eyes were wideset, and his lower jaw was recessive. His body was constructed with all the angularity of a whippet, but his legs were short—almost shorter than one would expect with a Jack Russell. His tail was long like a greyhound's, but if he let it down, it would quite literally drag behind him. His pelt, coloured like a Jack Russell's, seemed incapable of sitting flat and had the coarse, prickly consistency of a doormat.

"As long as Liam likes him," I said, "that's all that matters. Speak to the Tremblays, Mr. Hendrix, and figure out a schedule for veterinary and grooming excursions. You'll be responsible for taking him out on such errands."

"Yes sir," said Liam. He stepped forward and extended his hand to the animal. Hieronymus growled. "He's a bit touchy."

"Does he bite?" Paige asked

"I hope not," said Liam.

"He better not," said Paige.

Liam, the dog's lead in hand, walked out the back kitchen door into the garden.

Paige stepped close to my side as we watched the two leave. "What is its name again?"

I opened my phone to make sure I got it right. "Hieronymus," I read carefully.

"It suits him," she said.

The first meal the Peterkins took together after Dudley's return was a late lunch. Though it was a beautiful day, Amelia requested that I serve the meal in the dining room.

Dudley was in excellent spirits and wore another loud, patterned shirt, much like the one in the photo Paige had shown me. Amelia, however, seemed quiet and removed.

"Did you see that dog, Lancaster?"

"Yes sir."

"Holy cow. What a demon! Have you seen it, Amy?"

"No I haven't, Dudley."

"Brace yourself. It's nasty."

"Like that shirt?"

"This?" Dudley suddenly looked distressed. "You don't like it?"

Amelia laughed despite herself. "Dudley!"

"Well, I like it," he said, grinning rebelliously. "Lancaster?"

"Consider me a neutral party, sir."

"That means he hates it," said Amelia.

"Then he's definitely not going to like the other things I bought."

Amelia changed the subject. "How was the city?"

"Oh, it was pretty much how I left it. Made me miss being home."

Amelia pursed her lips. She glanced at me, perhaps wondering how much Paige was in the habit of sharing with me.

"Dudley," she said, "tell me about the art galleries."

"They were great," said Dudley. He glanced at me as well. "Loads of art. Speaking of which, we met a few gallery owners who seemed very interested in displaying Lucy's work."

"Really!"

"Yes. I invited them to come up and visit. I said we'd put them up in town and host a private little art show for them. A soirée, if you will."

"Will they end up living here as well?"

Dudley laughed. Amelia smiled, but did not laugh.

"No," said Dudley.

"When is this soirée?"

"Ah," said Dudley. "We were thinking Sunday."

"The day after tomorrow?"

"Yes."

Amelia nodded. "Lancaster?" Her voice was still quiet and even. "It seems we're hosting an art show here this weekend. Perhaps you'd better get started on that."

I took my leave.

At about four o'clock that afternoon, Dudley found me reading outside the warden's cottage. His brow was furrowed, and his ears were red. He was no longer wearing the shirt.

"Lancaster!"

I rose quickly. "Hello, Mr. Peterkin."

"Sorry for messing with your break, but I just want to apologise to you for springing this soirée thing on you."

"Not at all, sir. I have already talked with Miss Schopenhauer and preparations are well underway."

"Perfect! Thank you so much."

"My pleasure."

Dudley dawdled. He looked up at me a couple of times before he was able to get himself started. "Lancaster," he began, "I don't want burden you."

"Oh good."

"But the thing is, I think Amy might be mad at me."

"Surely not."

"I think she might be nervous about this new season of my life."

"Ah."

"Why are you doing that?"

"I beg your pardon, sir?"

"You just straightened your tie."

"Perhaps it was crooked."

"It wasn't."

"I'm relieved to hear it."

"Do you even know when you do this stuff? Whenever anyone tries to talk to you about anything personal, you stand at attention and start fixing your clothes. It's like a weird tic that only you would have." Dudley seemed genuinely annoyed.

"I'll try to be more conscious of it, sir."

"Why do I even bother trying? You won't talk about this kind of thing with me."

"I think it's for the best, sir."

Dudley turned and started walking back to the house. He stopped, and after a moment's consideration, half-turned toward me. "Sorry, Lancaster. And sorry again about the short notice for Sunday."

"Not at all, sir. I hope you will let me know if I can help you in any way."

"No. It's my fault. I'll sort it." He glanced back at me, making brief eye contact. "It would be great if I had somebody like you who I could talk to about stuff like this, Lancaster."

And then he left. I watched him go with a heavy heart.

(Saturday, April 16)

The Tremblays, in an oddly impotent gesture of hospitality, invited the Peterkins to join them for lunch on Saturday. To facilitate this generosity, the Peterkins' cook made a special meal, to be served in the Peterkins' house by the Peterkins' employees.

Lucian's sister, Diana Tremblay, was a member of the party. When I was in the kitchen helping Paige plate the lunch, she asked me to describe Diana. I somewhat absentmindedly replied that Diana looked as though she would be very hard to tip over.

"What the hell does that mean?" Paige interjected, pausing in her work to glare at me incredulously. "Do you mean she's short? Heavy?"

I pursed my lips and considered this question carefully. "Both, I suppose. Very low centre of gravity."

"Who rates people based on how tippable they look? How else would you describe her, you weirdo?"

"She looks divorced."

Paige narrowed her eyes. "You're messing with me."

"No, she really does."

"Okay, but what does that mean? I can't picture this person at all! All you've told me is that she appears to be a divorcee who's steady on her feet. What am I supposed to do with that?"

"She also looks older than Lucian. Definitely. Probably ten years or so."

"I wonder if he was the baby of the family."

That was something worth considering.

Though she had originally intended to fly back home Saturday evening, Diana Tremblay was now planning to stay an extra night or two. The woman was lingering. She repeatedly reminded people that caring for the Tremblays' dog had been a difficult business, and it was quite apparent that she mentioned it to justify the extension of her stay. It was also quite apparent that Diana was the only person unable to grasp the true dynamics of the lunch being "hosted" by Lucian and Kandyss.

"What an incredible meal," she sighed about halfway through the repast. "And what complex wine!" Before the gods of etiquette could get their hands on a lightning bolt, she turned to Amelia, and with a simper that could have been bottled and labeled *eau de gauche*, said, "Are you finding that having artists in the house is teaching you a thing or two about sophisticated living?"

I was standing at the periphery of the dining area, from which position I was able to make eye contact with Liam. He met my gaze eagerly, glad that he hadn't been the only one to hear the injudicious comment. We neither of us allowed our feelings to become visible on our faces, but there was joy in sharing the moment together nonetheless.

The climax of the meal arrived with the presentation of a gift from Lucian to Kandyss. It was not clear why he was giving her a gift in that moment, as the purpose of the luncheon was ostensibly to thank the Peterkins. However, with the main course removed and rumours of dessert keeping everyone seated at the table, Lucian excused himself only to return in a matter of seconds bearing a vertical, rectangular object draped in black cloth.

"While I was in New York with Dudley, I purchased a very special doodad and thought this was as good an occasion as any to present it to my Kandyss."

Diana Tremblay drew in her breath sharply, suggesting that she was delighted by her brother's romantic instincts.

Lucian placed this "doodad" at the head of the table and withdrew its shroud with a flourish. The object of interest was a stone tablet suspended within a frame of mottled brass. The stone looked old and weathered, but the markings on its face were clearly lines of Latin. From where I stood, the only thing I could make out clearly was "XI" carved in large numerals at the head of the stone.

I noticed that Amelia immediately leaned forward, squinting slightly as she tried to read the writing. It should go without saying that Latin was quite familiar to the woman.

Lucian also noted Amelia's attention. In fact, from where I stood, it appeared that it was Mrs. Peterkin's reaction he studied rather than that of Mrs. Tremblay. "Perhaps," he said, "you would like to tell Kandyss what we have here."

"I've no idea," said Amelia. "I can't read it from here."

"Oh?" Lucian was almost gleeful. "So you've not seen something like this before?"

"I don't know," said Amelia. "What is it?"

Lucian removed a sheet of paper from his pocket and unfolded it with something like ceremony. The artist cleared his throat and glanced about the room to make sure that he held everyone's attention. He saw me, and for a brief moment his good cheer was disrupted. I stared back at him evenly, and he looked down at his paper with a tiny scowl. Clearly, my presence had not been included in his earlier visualisations of this moment.

Now, I shall not pretend to have perfect recollection of all the details he read from that piece of paper. The claim was that this was part of a recreation of an ancient collection of laws written by the early Romans. The recreation was supposed to have been completed in Asia Minor during the thirteenth century. This tablet was allegedly the last remaining member of that original collection.

"Ha!" said Hoffman. This was the first comment the gentleman had seen fit to make for the entirety of the lunch.

"Dad!" remonstrated Amelia. She didn't make much of an effort.

"Found it on eBay, did you?" Hoffman asked. He issued a creaking, damp snort of laughter.

"This," said Lucian, smacking at the paper in his hand, "is a certificate of authenticity with a full record of provenance."

"I'm sure its provenance is excellent," said Amelia placatingly.

I knew nothing about such matters, but however little I knew, I was a leading authority when compared to Kandyss Tremblay. The happy recipient of what was allegedly an antiquity of significant value sat and looked affectedly thoughtful as she listened to Lucian read. Her face betrayed neither delight nor comprehension. She glanced about her to see if others were as confused as she was.

Others were. Because here was the thing: Kandyss knew nothing about medieval or Roman history, but Amelia Peterkin was a genuine expert.

My mind raced. What was I watching? Why would Lucian Tremblay present a gift to Kandyss that could afford the latter no pleasure whatsoever? Why would he choose a gift that was so specifically relevant to Amelia's work? I recalled suddenly that strange conversation wherein he had revealed his concern that Amelia wasn't taking him seriously. Was this whole lunch just an occasion to demonstrate, in an entirely offhand way, that he was the intellectual equal of those who paid for his living? When next I made eye contact with Liam, my brow was furrowed.

Amelia asked a host of questions about the stone. She was in no way critical, but I could tell she was bothered by it. Lucian received her questions with delight, eager to teach Amelia a thing or two on a subject where she should surely have been his superior.

Diana's smirk became so fixed that it might as well have been carved into her face like the lettering on the stone tablet.

Kandyss told Liam that she wanted dessert brought out and then contented herself with a mute, thoughtful examination of the tabletop.

"What the hell was that all about?" Liam asked a couple hours later as we were cleaning the vacant dining room.

I glanced at the back door to make sure that it was shut. The Peterkins and Tremblays had decided to take their conversation onto the veranda, where they could enjoy some fresh air. The only member of the household who had declined the opportunity to socialise was Hoffman. It was my belief that he had now retired for a nap, as was his custom following a hearty lunch.

"What are you asking about?" I replied. "The lunch or the gift?"

"That stone," Liam stripped the cloth from the sideboard we had used with an expert twist. "I felt like I was missing something the entire time. Was it supposed to be symbolic? Ka—Mrs. Tremblay didn't seem all that impressed, and it kind of seemed like a weird gesture in the middle of a lunch where they're supposed to be thanking the Peterkins."

"I have no idea," I replied, feigning disinterest.

I was still mulling over the events of lunch when I served the Peterkins their supper that evening.

So was Amelia.

"Dud," she said, "there is no way that stone is what he says it is."

The possibility of the stone being inauthentic did not appear to have occurred to Dudley. "Oh?" he cried with sincere surprise. "Why?"

"Look who has it," snorted Hoffman. "Do you seriously think those soup-dribblers could avoid being defrauded?"

"Oh Dad," said Dudley affably. He was not as good at scolding Hoffman as Amelia.

"It's just..." Amelia struggled to find words that captured the magnitude of her complaint. "I read its provenance. I can't say exactly why, but it's setting off some alarm bells. Besides, if such a thing did exist, I would be a little surprised that I had never even heard of it."

"Oh well," said Dudley. "I just hope that Lucifer didn't spend too much money on it. As long as it was cheap, who cares? I doubt Kandyss will."

"Still," said Amelia. "It seems kind of outrageous to just let it go. Maybe I can convince them to seek further authentication?"

"What if it *is* authentic?" asked Dudley.

"Then it should probably be sent to a museum in Turkey."

"Well..." began Dudley.

"It's not authentic, Dudley."

"Right."

I watched the evening sun set behind vineyard-covered hills. Purple shadows advanced between the rows of grapevines like slow-dancing spirits celebrating the passing of another day.

There was a splash and a glug as Hoffman emptied the bottle into his glass. I glanced down at my own drink, trying to gauge whether I would need to go get another bottle. There was still plenty in my glass, and as I swirled it, I watched the sunset's bright hues reflected in the port's rich, tawny lustre.

"Did you hear that man's sister at lunch?" Hoffman asked.

I glanced at my employer's parent and saw how intently he watched me. It was in moments of intelligent focus like this that I wondered how others could think him senile. I looked back at the horizon and nodded.

Hoffman grunted and tapped an arrhythmic tattoo into the stone ledge with his fingertips. “They won’t last long,” he said. “It simply won’t work out.”

I allowed myself to glance at the old man once more. He had said those words before, but this time he spoke with less hopefulness and more resolve. He had joined me in watching the sunset, and I observed that his jaw was clenched.

I looked back at the vineyards just in time to see a hawk glide effortlessly across the mauve sky. I drank my port and focused on its radiant warmth flooding my being.

(Sunday, April 17)

The soirée in honour of Lucian Tremblay’s art was held in the West Wing. There were three large doorways with double doors and gothic arches that could open up the wall between the Peterkins’ dining room and the larger sitting area. The resulting space was substantial, allowing for plenty of movement and little pockets of semi-privacy—ideal for a mingling party.

There were to be three gallery curators and a host of Lucian’s artist friends joining us for the evening. Diana Tremblay, unsurprisingly, decided to stick around to support her brother. Much more surprising was Patrick Hoffman’s expressed desire to be present.

“Wouldn’t miss it for the world,” he said happily as he watched Liam and me moving furniture about under the supervision of Amelia.

“Why is that, Dad?” Amelia sounded just a little nervous at her father’s enthusiasm.

"I remember one time," said Hoffman in his typical narrative voice, "a reception being held at an embassy to celebrate the arrival of a new ambassador in the city. Loads of fancy people invited. The ambassador, Rainier, got flattened by a truck within minutes of leaving the airport. In the excitement of the moment, nobody remembered to cancel the party. Guests started pouring in, and the caterer was there, faithfully filling their troughs. Everyone wanted to meet the new ambassador, but he was on ice at the police station, waiting to fly back home."

"Dad," said Amelia, "that's a horrible story! Why would you tell that story?"

"Oh," said Hoffman, "I would have thought the comparison was obvious. A party for an ambassador who's not there? A bunch of people showing up for an art show that hasn't got any paintings?"

And that *was* an interesting dynamic of the evening. Since moving in, Lucian had been waiting for a friend back home to get his paintings out of storage and send them to Harper's Lane. Almost two weeks had passed, and those paintings were still nowhere to be seen. Whether this was because Lucian forgot or because his friend was indolent or because getting paintings out of storage is somehow more difficult than I imagine it being, they remained safely stashed away in a rental unit in a faraway city.

However, to say that there would be no paintings was a slight exaggeration. Lucian did have two canvases that he had brought from their last residence when they moved in. They were both pieces Dudley had seen at the fundraiser where he first met Lucian, and the artist maintained that they were representative of his work as a whole. To relieve the peculiarity of an art showing with only two pieces, Dudley got Lucian to put together an album of good photographs of his other paintings. These images would be cast on one of the walls during the evening by a ceiling-mounted projector.

Such matters did not, however, concern us domestics. For Liam and me, preparations were primarily focused on ensuring a steady flow of drinks and nibblies. Paige had prepared a generous quantity of tapas, and they were arrayed across the entire length of the dining room table on trays that we could circulate if necessary. We had several wines standing by for pouring and an army of polished glasses twinkling on the sideboard.

The guests started arriving shortly after eight.

"Feeling ready?" Liam asked me as we watched the first car pull up the drive and park along the side of the house. It was one of those little convertible Mercedes that can only be driven by card-carrying members of the International Society of Complete Plonkers.

I opened the door as the guests started mounting the steps. "Yes," I said. "As ready as I'll ever be." It was a cliché, but one that aptly described my feeling of preparedness. Everything material was in order, yet I anticipated the evening's events with a certain dread.

The first arrival was the director of a gallery called The Grant. I know, because that's how he introduced himself to everyone the entire night. He was a big, loud man who seemed habituated to bludgeoning people with his voice. He beamed at me as I held the door open for him.

"Thank you, Jeeves!" he bellowed. Spying Liam, who was holding a tray of champagne, he bustled over and took a flute in each hand. "There you are, darling," he said, extending one of the drinks to the slender woman who shadowed him closely.

Amelia joined us and introductions were made.

The director's name was Bryce McNab, and the willowy creature flickering silently in his wake turned out to be his daughter, who worked at the same gallery. The possibility that the gallery curators would be bringing guests of their own had not been discussed by the Peterkins.

"Will you have enough of everything if there are more people bringing entourages?" asked Amelia in a hushed voice as soon as these guests had been led away by Lucian.

"Yes ma'am."

I glanced at Amelia and wondered how she felt about the evening's invasion. She couldn't have been thrilled about it, but her face wore no evidence of disapprobation. Her composure was immaculate.

"I didn't anticipate extras," she said quietly.

"I always anticipate extras."

"That's why you're the butler." She patted my arm. "Thank you, Lancaster. Let me know if you need anything at any point tonight. Between us, I don't know what to expect."

"I can sympathise with that sentiment."

"Here we go," she said, observing a couple more vehicles pulling into the drive.

The second of the curators came alone. The third, the owner of a boutique gallery with a small staff, had magnanimously invited her entire team. These, in addition to the ragtag horde of Lucian's close artistic friends, brought the guest count to twenty-one. Even when that number was combined with the household occupants, I was not concerned. We were armed with a great supply of food and drink, and it was still a relatively small party.

The evening began quite smoothly. Once everyone had arrived, Dudley Peterkin stood up and tapped his glass with a pen, gathering the room's attention. My employer was wearing a brown suede shirt and white jeans. He looked as though he was himself a frustrated artist. I felt a wave of embarrassment on his behalf as he said a few words about how he had met Lucian and how pleased he was to be involved in the career of so promising an artist. He then asked Lucian to share some thoughts on the vision and ethos of his art.

"Maybe just take a few minutes," said Dudley, "and guide us into your central project like you did for me back in February."

Lucian Tremblay began talking. I refuse to recount any of what I heard him say. If Lucian had one quality, it was the ability to share thoughts on his vision. He could talk drivel for days without pausing for love of water or air.

Liam and I stayed busy throughout the ensuing speech passing trays of tapas and refreshing drinks. Things were still going quite well, as far as I could tell. The only difficulty that had surfaced so far had to do with a couple of the staff from the boutique gallery who seemed to be living their very own rock-and-roll art gallery lifestyle and were manifesting this wildness by trying to sneak off together to satisfy some unspeakable range of animal urges. I caught them halfway up the stairs to the West Wing upper hall.

"Pardon me."

"Oh!" The young lady yipped. "Hi!"

They looked guiltily at one another and shared a giggle.

"Is there something I can help you find?"

"No, no. We're good. Just exploring," said the young man.

"I must ask that you limit your exploration to the main rooms that you'll find behind me. This is a private residence."

"Sorry."

The young lady seemed bolder than her admirer. "We were hoping to find somewhere quiet where we can talk. That room down there is so full and loud."

I considered being sarcastic but remembered my station. "Come now," I said. "You wouldn't want to miss Mr. Tremblay's presentation."

"We would!" the young man said bitterly. "It's awful."

I couldn't help but sympathise with that sentiment.

The first indication that the evening was going to become truly interesting was the intoxication of Diana Tremblay. She was using the food table to remain upright when I came over to see that it was still well-stocked.

"What's your name again, cutie?"

"Lancaster, ma'am."

"You know who I am?"

"I do have that pleasure, yes."

"Say my name."

"I beg your pardon?"

"I like the way you talk."

"Thank you, ma'am. May I recommend that you take a seat for a few minutes? The evening seems to be wearing on you. You may be able to collect yourself with a little rest."

"I'm fine."

"I'm pleased to hear it."

For a moment Diana stopped talking and gazed passively at my waistcoat. She had apparently fallen into a meditative trance. Despite what I had told Paige when describing Diana a week earlier, I reflected that this woman could very easily tip over in her current condition. I was about to take advantage of her lapse in consciousness and slip away when she came to with a start.

"There!" she barked. It was as if someone was adjusting the rabbit ears on her television and the picture had suddenly come into focus. She looked at me and took a moment to recall where we had left things. It didn't take her long. She put on her naughtiest smile. "Say my name," she said hungrily.

"Would you excuse me, ma'am?"

"You don't know it, do you?" She tilted closer and pressed herself against my left side. "It's *Diana!"* She pronounced her own name like a euphemism.

I stepped back, and she almost fell to the floor.

"Goodness," I said. I took my leave without further ceremony, carefully brushing off my left coat sleeve.

I found Liam, and we stood together by the wall, watching the crowd for empty glasses. Most of the party stood in a knot around Lucian, who was discussing the different paintings that appeared on the projected slideshow. There were also outliers: a small number of persons who seemed less interested in the evening's purpose. Diana, for instance, was by the dining table dissecting a caprese spoon with great care. The gallery curator who had come without any guests was slumped in an armchair next to Patrick Hoffman, and the pair were deep in conversation. The two staff members who had been trying to sneak upstairs were flirting ravenously behind a large ficus, oblivious to their surroundings.

Liam tilted his head in my direction and spoke in a discreet undertone. "I noticed that you have the attention of Mr. Tremblay's sister."

"Oh, you noticed that, did you?"

"Hard to miss."

The amorous couple broke from the cover of their ficus like a pair of rabbits and made for the kitchen door.

"Mr. Hendrix," I said, "would you please head off Romeo and Juliet?"

"Gladly."

The underbutler maneuvered through the crowd and disappeared into the kitchen right behind the couple. I pitied him.

"Lancaster!" Kandyss Tremblay had slipped away from Lucian's thrall and was approaching. She had Bryce McNab in tow.

"Mrs. Tremblay," I greeted her.

"Get me and Bryce some more champagne? Pleeeease?"

"Certainly ma'am."

"Hop to it, Jeeves!" boomed McNab.

As I set off on my errand, the not unlikely pair dropped themselves onto a sofa. I returned to find Kandyss showing McNab something on her phone. I lowered my tray to allow them to take the champagne.

McNab looked at me warily as he took both the drinks. He passed Kandyss her drink as he had done for his daughter when he arrived. His eyes returned to mine, and his expression was almost hostile. I could see that he was trying to decide if I was judging him. In my experience, the only people who worry about being judged by me are misbehaving.

"That'll be all," said McNab shortly.

"Thank you, sir," I said.

I returned to my former post and immediately wished I had found a new one. The voices of Kandyss and McNab were clearly audible from where I stood.

"So this is what you do?" barked McNab in his outrageous voice. "My kind of art!"

I wondered where the man's daughter had got to.

"These are just some different takes from one of my recent product promotions," said Kandyss grandly. "Oops! Don't look at that. I was just checking my makeup before a take, and I didn't realise the phone was recording. Here. I'm going to delete it right now. Oops. No. No!"

In a single, wonderful moment the slideshow of Lucian Tremblay's art on the wall flickered and vanished. It was replaced by a huge, bright video of Kandyss Tremblay puckering her lips at the camera. She must have been a mere couple of inches from her phone when she shot the video, because her face was at no time entirely visible in the frame.

In some rooms this would have resulted in an eruption of laughter. Such was not the case here. Several people tittered awkwardly, but most just glanced in horror between Lucian and Kandyss. The only person who was not made uncomfortable by the moment appeared to be Hoffman, who was slapping his knee in a paroxysm of hearty approval.

“Kandyss?” Lucian called out.

“Sorry! I accidentally hit the little cast button. I don’t know how to turn it off!”

The video paused. Then it started over again from the beginning. Then it paused. Then it played. The tittering grew in intensity and membership. It was a good minute or two before the error was corrected and Lucian was able to resume discussing his paintings.

“Where was I?” he asked, his face red. He quickly succeeded in resurrecting the respectful attention of his audience.

“That wasn’t my fault,” Kandyss explained to McNab in a quieter voice than before. “I thought the cast button was the delete button for a minute.”

McNab muttered something reassuring. He seemed to have been embarrassed by the incident, but not enough to stop flirting with Lucian’s wife.

Bastard.

I was suddenly conscious of a narrow, wispy person standing perfectly still beside my elbow. “I beg your pardon," I said hastily, "may I assist you?"

The young woman, whom I recognised as Bryce McNab's daughter, smiled cheerfully at me. Her big glasses sat so high up on her nose that it looked like she was peeking over the bottom of the frame. "No," she said. "I'm good." Her voice was soft but not awkward.

"You're certain?"

She nodded. It appeared that she was content to stand very close by me and join me in watching the room. I wondered if she was seeking conversation or merely taking refuge in the quiet dignity of my shadow. I have had that effect before.

"There you are, Stirling!" cried Diana. She was pointing at me from across the room.

I saw Amelia Peterkin look over at me with an expression of surprise and concern. I gave her a reassuring shrug. Poor Amelia had enough to worry about without having to come to my rescue.

"Is your name Stirling?" McNab's daughter asked.

"No."

Together we watched Diana approaching me. Her progress was slow and unsteady, but she kept looking up and grinning at me to remind herself that the journey was worthwhile.

"I didn't think so. I thought I heard someone call you Lancaster."

"That's right."

"My name's Melody."

"It's a pleasure to meet you," I said, nodding at her respectfully.

She nodded in turn and lapsed back into a contented silence. Considering her parentage, this young woman possessed a surprisingly pleasant, honest friendliness. She reminded me in a small way of Dudley Peterkin. At least—I looked up at the gaudy figure who was nodding and scowling with concentration at Lucian's drivel—she reminded me of Dudley as I liked to remember him.

Diana reached us at last. She looked Melody up and down with disgust. "Screw off, Sissy," she said. Then she caught herself, realised that this was not a polite greeting, and tried again. "Sorry," she said. "Now go find someone your own size." At this juncture she saw fit to bob her eyebrows at me.

My skin crawled.

"It was nice to meet you, Lancaster," said Melody.

"A mutual pleasure, Melody," I said.

The young woman took her leave.

"Ha! So you can say *her* name!" Diana wagged her finger at me. "You're a naughty, naughty man, Vickers." She swallowed effortfully and blinked.

"Ms. Tremblay," I said, "may I recommend that you retire for the evening? It is my opinion that you have made a very good impression tonight, and it may be just as well to leave others wanting more."

Diana stood before me in perfect silence, staring hard at my mouth and rocking gently back and forth. She seemed to be considering my words very seriously indeed. Finally, she cocked her head to one side and asked, "What did you say?"

"I think..." My words died on my lips as her hand found my thigh. I pulled back and struck the wall behind me. “Remember yourself!” I said sternly.

“Naughty!” she chirped.

I became uncomfortably conscious that Diana Tremblay’s inebriated courtship ritual was being watched by a number of the party guests. Being on the receiving end of such attentions always makes one wonder how the interaction is being perceived. Did onlookers consider it possible that there was a degree of mutuality in the exchange? Was I seen as encouraging or failing to adequately discourage the amorous advances of my suitor?

I decided to simplify things. “Ms. Tremblay,” I said. “Diana.”

“Oooh!”

“I think you ought to go to bed.”

“Oh you do, do you?” she leered suggestively. She tried to look me up and down but almost lost her balance. “You gonna help me get there, Whitley?”

I was about to reply when a loud guffaw from Bryce McNab cut me short. Apparently Kandyss had managed to be funny.

Diana scowled at the pair. “Look at that bimbo,” she muttered darkly.

“Now, now,” I said quickly. “Let’s not forget ourselves.”

“Sitting there—” Diana teetered. “Sitting there,” she started again, “like she belongs. Worst mistake my brother ever made.”

“What did you just say?” Kandyss had apparently been listening.

“Oh!” hooted Diana eloquently. “Yeah!”

“Hey, hey, hey!” For Amelia to cross the room was the work of a moment. She towered between the women like an elegant goddess preparing to dispense justice. "You feeling okay, Diana?"

"Fine. Just trying to have a private conversation with B-B-Barracuda here and Kandyss is..." she ran out of steam and teetered, trying to aim an accusing finger at Kandyss's face.

"Lancaster," said Amelia in a fine, authoritative voice, "you can go. I'll take Diana to her room."

"I'm fine," said Diana loudly.

The room had become quieter, and a growing number of eyes were indelicately drinking in the sight of a drunk woman arguing with the hostess. Lucian was somehow looking paler than usual.

"No, you're not," said Amelia firmly. "You're drunk and making a scene. Let's go."

And Diana didn't argue, because Amelia wasn't using a voice with which one is able to argue. Mumbling feeble, emotional complaints, she let Amelia guide her from the room.

Feeling winded by the exchange, I decided to go to the kitchen for a drink of water. I was almost at the door when it opened, and Liam appeared.

"Did they come back through here?" he asked.

And I realised that it was time for our next problem. I waved the underbutler back into the kitchen and shut the door behind us. First things first. I filled a mug with water and drank deeply. Then I took a deep breath and faced Liam.

"You didn't catch them?"

"No," he said bitterly. "They were faster than I expected."

"Do you have any idea where they went?"

"No. I've looked everywhere. I think they went outside, but I can't find them in the gardens. I think they probably went back into the house by a different door."

I took another sip of water and looked out the kitchen door to the lawns beyond. "That pair could be anywhere at this point," I said.

"Anywhere at all," Liam agreed.

"Doing things," I said.

My bitter reverie was interrupted by a sharp sound emanating through the door to the dining room. It was unmistakably the sound of a dog barking, yet Hieronymus had been shut up in the Tremblays' bedroom.

"Oh no," said Liam. "I think I know where those people went."

"Mr. Hendrix," I said, "go at once and chase them out. Chase them clear off the property if necessary. I'll take care of matters in here." I adjusted my tie and strode back out of the kitchen.

When I rejoined the soirée, I found that every last person present was standing stock still and staring at Hieronymus. This is not a normal reaction for most people upon beholding a dog. Normally, people coo and smile and try to pet a dog when it enters a room. However, as already mentioned, Hieronymus was not a normal-looking dog. No doubt the guests were wondering how this hellish, badger–wolf crossbreed had gotten into the house. The common theme among the expressions visible from where I stood was one of revulsion.

"Aha!" said Lucian. "This is our dog, Hieronymus."

There were some chuckles and comments about the name, but nobody rushed forward to interact with the animal.

Hieronymus, for his part, was studying the room in a manner that very much reminded me of an acquaintance of mine. I had met this person when working at a property on the Riviera for a period of eighteen months. The gentleman in question had been a little under two years of age at the time and very given to antisocial behaviour. He would often enter rooms with just such a posture as Hieronymus now assumed. Just like Hieronymus, he would scan the room with a lazy, insolent eye, sizing up the fighting potential of its every inhabitant. Then, his research complete, the little fellow would variously break something or bite someone. Sometimes he did both.

"How did he get out?" Lucian asked. "Kandyss?"

"Huh?" Kandyss had been listening to a mumbled monologue from McNab when her husband spoke. She seemed a little disoriented. "What did you say?"

"Did you let him out?"

"Who?"

And then Lucian became quite rude. Though I am not inclined to express any sympathy for the man in general terms, I will concede that the evening must have been somewhat taxing for him. Two out of the three gallery curators were ignoring his discussion of paintings. His wife, who seemed to be all that one of the so-called curators showed any interest in, had hijacked his slideshow presentation with her silly video. His sister had gotten drunk and made a scene. Now their rabid fever dream of a pet had appeared and was mere moments away from hunting gallery curators for sport.

"The dog, Kan! That! There! What the hell do you think I'm talking about, you stupid woman?"

Like I said. Rude.

Kandyss was on her feet in an instant. "How dare you!" she shrieked. "You know how much I hate it when you call me that! I've told you and told you and told you! How *dare* you?"

When Lucian spoke again, he wasn't shouting, but he wasn't talking quietly either. It was just that perfect volume that requires anyone trying to cut you off to do the shouting instead. "You know," he said, "I think maybe you should go to bed as well. You and Diana have both had enough fun for one night."

"You *jerk!"* she cried.

They continued to fling mud at one another loudly and with no thought for the rest of the guests' experience. It was at this point, however, that I stopped listening. My attention was on Hieronymus. The dog's wideset, ghoulish eyes were sparkling with delight as he observed his owners screaming at one another. It is my belief that he knew they were distracted and that his time had come.

"Oh dear," I said.

In a flash of flailing, ungainly limbs, the dog was on the furniture. He leapt from sofa to sofa to table to chair as if playing a game of "The Floor Is Lava." As he went, drinks, guests, and objets d'art were thrown to the floor.

Above the din I heard Hoffman thundering loud and colourful obscenities at the dog. I seem to recall him throwing things at the animal, but I couldn't swear to it. There were lots of things flying at that point for lots of reasons.

Lucian and Kandyss were apparently oblivious to their dog's behaviour and continued to openly discuss their mutual contempt at increasing volume as the room fell into true and complete chaos.

The evening's denouement was bizarre but brief. All the guests saw clearly that it was time to go and did so quietly and quickly.

"It was good to meet you, Lancaster," said Melody.

"Likewise," I said.

"I think I'd like being a butler."

"I think you might."

And then she was gone. She was followed by the rest of guests, including the two blushing miscreants Liam chased out of the Tremblays' quarters. They filed down the front steps, clambered into their various cars, and sped off into the night, leaving us to pick up the pieces.

Lucian and Kandyss retired for the evening, dragging a gleeful Hieronymus.

Liam and I, with some help from the Peterkins, cleaned up the house.

"Artists are very *different,*" said Dudley, sweeping up broken glass with a grim expression on his face.

"Some are, anyway," agreed his wife.

Neither of the Peterkins seemed pleased with how the evening had gone, but Hoffman, sitting in the corner with his mug of tea, was positively thrilled.

* * *

Diana Tremblay flew out the next morning, never to return.

On Tuesday, Lucian Tremblay's art and supplies finally arrived. Up until that time, he had not demonstrated in any way that his was the life of an artist. He had enjoyed access to a large study in the East Wing that had been set aside for the purpose of a studio. It had been selected for its giant, south-facing windows that could maximise the artist's access to natural light. Yet for all that, the room had remained entirely neglected for the two weeks that the Tremblays had lived at Harper's Lane.

Just after ten o'clock that morning, a van stopped in front of the house, and two men alighted. They wore uniforms indicating that they were employed by a moving company. They didn't approach the house, so I began to approach them. They were busy lighting cigarettes when I hailed them, and they both hastily rubbed out their lights on the van's flank.

"Gentlemen!" I called. "May I—"

And then I saw Lucian Tremblay's car pulling into the drive behind them.

The taller of the two men pointed to Lucian by way of explanation, and I nodded. Together, no words being exchanged, the three of us waited for Tremblay to make his intentions known.

"Lancaster!"

"Mr. Tremblay."

"Get Liam out here."

I nodded. "Very good, sir. Is there some way in which you require Mr. Hendrix and me to assist you?"

Lucian sneered. My referring to the underbutler as "Mr. Hendrix" immediately after he had utilised the young man's given name was being taken as a correction.

"I need this van unloaded," he said.

I glanced at the two movers.

Lucian rightly understood the question in my eyes. "These two donkeys aren't touching another one of my paintings," he said. "They already did enough damage loading them into the van at the airport."

The two men exchanged a look more expressive of exasperation than remorse.

"I'll have Mr. Hendrix join us at once," I said. I removed myself to an appropriate distance before taking out my phone and calling the underbutler.

Moving art, I learned, requires two things. It requires a pair of household domestics in shirtsleeves carefully carrying every piece between them (regardless of the size of the canvas). Also essential is a supervisor who treats those same domestics as if they are hardened criminals whose only aim is the savage destruction of all art.

Quite early in the proceedings, I made the mistake of picking up a painting alone, setting out to carry its full three feet by four toward the house.

"Lancaster!" Lucian cried in distress. "What are you doing?"

I was genuinely confused. I lowered the painting so I could look at him over the top of it. "Sir?"

"Together!" He was pleading, desperately, as if for mercy. *"Together!"*

Liam came over and silently took one end of the painting while I took the other. Together the two of us carried that burden of several pounds into the house, avoiding eye contact with one another and remaining entirely mute lest any honest thought should escape us. Lucian followed closely, offering invaluable advice as to how we might better hold the canvas and shouting whenever we came within six feet of walls, doorways, or potted plants. He also held doors for us as we made the long, soul-cleansing pilgrimage to the East Wing studio. His stertorous, near-panicked breathing filled our ears like the roar of coastal breakers.

Whenever we were outside, our work was watched by the two movers who sat in the shade, smoking incessantly. Whenever Liam or I made eye contact with these professionals, we were graced with expressions of deep sympathy. I felt like a young draftee being saluted by old veterans.

Whenever we were inside, it was Lucian who enjoyed sympathetic attention. As he sweated and panted between bouts of squealing at us for our various attempts at destroying his life's work, his supportive wife stroked his arm and cooed gently in his ear. She occasionally saw fit to join her husband in giving us advice, generally by informing us of the value of each piece. By her estimation, the collection could only have been exchanged for all the bullion in Fort Knox if discounted generously.

The highlight of the morning involved the introduction of Hieronymus into the project. He had been shut up in one of the bathrooms initially, but Kandyss apparently forgot this and accidentally let him out.

"Harry!" cried the woman.

I had not yet heard the Tremblays' nickname for their pet, and for a very brief moment I wondered who Harry might be. This fog was cleared by a white flash of pain as the teeth of the animal sank into my thigh.

"Don't drop it!" Lucian bellowed as I staggered forward, nearly pitching both painting and Liam through the door of the studio.

I don't know why Hieronymus chose to bite my thigh rather than my ankle. Perhaps his ancient hunting instincts told him that butlers cannot be merely harried—they must be brought down. Due to the length of his legs, the noble hound had been obliged to leap to get at my upper trouser region, and he now hung there limply, like a giant, snarling leech.

I had first staggered forward, as previously mentioned. Now, with this apex predator dragging me from behind and Liam pushing against the painting in an attempt to remain on his feet, I found myself sprinting backward. Together Hieronymus and I struck a small hallway table with enough force to dislodge the animal from my leg. He wriggled out from between me and the table, whining like a jackal. He padded a short distance away and then turned once more upon his prey, crouching in preparation for another attack.

My own ancient instincts burst to the forefront. With the nimbleness of an ibex, I sprang upon the table behind me, the painting we had been carrying somehow still cradled in my arms.

Lucian Tremblay made a strangled sound.

"Harry!" shrieked Kandyss.

Hieronymus started baying and scratching at the table's legs furiously. His prey was treed and only wanted some encouragement to come back down and fight like a man.

"Mr. Hendrix," I said firmly. "Collect this animal at once and return it to the bathroom."

Liam didn't need to be told twice. He dove at Hieronymus. The dog leapt lightly aside and continued levelling his verbal abuses at me while evading this new player.

"Don't drop it!" roared Lucian.

"I won't drop it!" I replied, very nearly shouting. "Now get that dog under control!"

"Harry!" wailed Kandyss.

Lucian joined Liam in trying to get a hand on Hieronymus. The dog was apparently channelling a hero in his ancestry and navigated the room expertly, teasing and dodging the two men effortlessly. All the while, he barraged me with a mocking tirade of snarls and barks.

Kandyss, in a moment of inspiration, produced a rubber toy that looked like a snowman. "Harry!" she called. The dog didn't appear to hear her. "Fetch!" she cried in an oddly guttural tone. Without apparently considering her surroundings, she whipped the toy down the hall, knocking a mirror from the wall and adding a minefield of broken glass to the fray.

I looked at Kandyss, and she looked back at me. Her expression was one of dismay mingled with outrage. I suspected in that moment that she considered me largely responsible for the present state of affairs.

Liam finally got hold of the dog's collar, bringing the madness to a conclusion.

"Oh no! Gentle!" cried Kandyss.

Lucian did not support his wife's concern for the animal. "Get that maggot out of here before I kill it," he said darkly. Turning to me, he held out his arms. "Give," he ordered.

I passed him the painting that I had held faithfully aloft. He took it and carried it into the studio, mute with fury. I descended from my perch without aid from either Tremblay.

"Are you all right, Mr. Lancaster?" Liam was back from incarcerating Hieronymus.

"I believe so," I said. I patted the back of my thigh gingerly. The trouser leg was damp, but I suspected that it was the animal's saliva rather than my blood that I felt.

Lucian emerged from his studio, took a deep breath, and asked how I was.

"Thank you for asking," I said stiffly. "I am sure that I will survive. However, in light of what has just occurred, I wonder if I should be concerned about the safety of our staff or guests."

"Why?" snapped Lucian.

"The dog Hieronymus just bit me."

"Did he?" Lucian shrugged. "Don't worry about it."

"I am responsible for the welfare of the staff here," I said. "It may be—"

Lucian held up a hand. "I told you not to worry about it," he said. His tone was that of a man who has been pushed beyond his limit and must, reluctantly, become authoritative. The hand that he had raised to silence me now pointed to the door. "There are still a few more canvases and all the materials still," he said, clapping impatiently for emphasis. "Let's go."

"He bit you?" cried Paige with feeling. She slipped off the counter onto her feet. "Poor Mr. Lancaster! Are you okay?"

"I believe so," I replied. I felt at the back of my trouser leg again. It throbbed and was quite tender to the touch.

"Let me have a look," said Paige.

"Oh no," I replied.

"Oh yes," she insisted. She advanced as if preparing to strong-arm me into submitting to her care.

"I really don't think it's necessary," I said. "Besides. I can't go letting my trousers down in your kitchen."

"You can if you try." She had the kitchen first aid box out and was arranging its contents on the counter as though preparing to play triage nurse to an entire battlefield. "Now stop making this weird, Mr. Lancaster, and show me your leg."

Mr. Hendrix entered a minute later and emitted a sharp "Ho!" of surprise at the sight of Paige inspecting my wounds. He turned away instinctively as if avoiding the sight of an indecency.

"Mr. Hendrix!" I barked. "Has that dog bitten you?" I spoke with greater force than was my custom. This was partly out of embarrassment, I suppose, and an effort to insist upon the normalcy of the scene.

"No," said Liam. He drew nearer, craning to see the wound on my thigh.

"Resist the urges of your morbid curiosity," I snapped.

"Right."

"Miss Schopenhauer?"

"It's bruised," said Paige, "but the skin doesn't look broken at all."

I straightened, grabbing at my trousers. "Then we're done here," I said. "Thank goodness for blunt teeth."

The kitchen door opened, and Amelia Peterkin entered.

"Ho!" said Liam again.

I folded my hands in front of my trousers, disguising effectively the fact that they were not fastened.

"Has someone been hurt?" Amelia asked. She had observed the open first aid kit.

"Not at all," I said hastily.

"Yes," said Paige.

Liam, standing beside and slightly behind Mrs. Peterkin, watched me with wide eyes.

Amelia tilted her head thoughtfully. "Well, that's not suspicious at all," she said with a soft, sarcastic drawl. "Lancaster, I heard that the Tremblays got you and Liam to unload the art today."

"That's right," I said. I felt my trousers slip ever so slightly and leaned against the counter behind me to hold them where they were. I would not normally lean like this in front of Mrs. Peterkin. I hoped that I appeared nonchalant but doubted that my hands clasped in front of me supported that illusion. Liam's expression confirmed my fears.

"Did we not hire movers with the van?"

"It was Mr. Tremblay's belief that they did not show enough care for the art," I said. "He hoped that Mr. Hendrix and I would be better able to meet his standards."

Amelia Peterkin wasn't smiling. "And did you?"

"I hope so," I said. I tried to shift myself into a more natural position.

"The fact is," said Liam, moving into Amelia's field of vision, "Mr. Tremblay's standards are not easily met."

Amelia turned to Liam and gave him her full attention. "I hope he was civil," she said.

"He wasn't at his best," said Liam. He then launched into a detailed description of the morning's antics, omitting only the scene with Hieronymus.

Paige's hand slid along the counter and grabbed the back of my trousers, pulling them up for me. I hastily pulled up the zipper of my fly, thus securing them well enough to allow me to straighten up.

Amelia was listening intently to Liam. "It sounds a bit stressful," she said.

"Mr. Tremblay did appear to find it so," I said.

Amelia nodded, as if some suspicion of hers had been confirmed. "Lancaster. Liam. I want to thank you for assisting the Tremblays in this way. If they ever seem to be taking advantage of your services, I want you to let either myself or Mr. Peterkin know right away."

"Thank you," I said.

"Is that a yes, Lancaster?" she asked sternly.

I smiled. “I appreciate your concern for our welfare, Mrs. Peterkin. I’m sure that we wouldn’t want to keep anything from you.”

“I’m going to call that a yes,” said Amelia, “and hold you to it.” She turned to leave.

Paige, who had been watching these proceedings with a savagely insolent eye, made a sound of disgust that halted our employer in her steps.

“Paige?”

“The Tremblays’ dog bit Lancaster.”

“I see,” said Amelia. She looked at me reprovingly. “That explains the first aid kit. It also explains why Lancaster’s pants aren’t buttoned.”

I hastily remedied the latter.

“Are you okay?” Amelia asked. Her concern was mingled with anger.

“I am.”

“Are you lying again?”

I felt myself stiffen to the point of paralysis. “I am not. The area is bruised, but the skin was unbroken. I will pull through.” The last sentence was an attempt at humour. I smiled lamely.

Amelia did not match my smile. She nodded, turned and left.

“Are you in trouble?” Liam asked, his expression concerned.

“It’s not possible for Lancaster to be in trouble,” said Paige. “But the Tremblays are finished.”

The Tremblays were not finished. I cannot say what sort of conversation took place between them and the Peterkins on the subject, but it did not result in anyone, human or canine, being "finished."

Dudley Peterkin addressed me on the subject over dinner. Mr. Hoffman had retired early, and so it was just the three of us.

"Lancaster," said Dudley, "We've got to clear up some stuff."

I stood at my regular station, feeling more passionate about stiff formality than usual and taking care not to brush the back of my left leg against the credenza. I said, "Sir?", and observing that Amelia's water glass ran low, advanced on the table with pitcher in hand.

"We have invited the Tremblays to stay with us. This is the first time I have made a real contribution to the arts, and it is overdue. I want this relationship to succeed." Dudley paused as I poured and resumed his speech as I returned to my station. "In hindsight, I think I was hasty in inviting the Tremblays to actually live with us without getting to know them better. If I could do it over, I wouldn't invite them to live here. I would probably offer a different kind of support."

"To say the least," said Amelia. She was watching her husband with an irritated expression.

"But now," continued Dudley, "I've put us in an awkward situation. The Tremblays have given up their previous home to come live with us. There might be growing pains, and there might be some transitional discomfort. However, it would be a real dick move to get them to fly their entire life here and then kick them out after two weeks because we didn't get along. That would really be on us. It would be a terrible thing to do to someone."

"However," prompted Amelia.

"However," said Dudley, *"if* this whole idea was a big mistake, I have to limit its effects. You've got to let us know if there's any more mistreatment from the Tremblays."

"Or their dog."

"Or, like Amelia says, their dog. You've got to tell me right away, Lancaster. If I'm out, text me. I have to know. I've told Lucifer that if his dog so much as growls at a member of the staff again, it'll be sent back to his sister immediately. You and Mr. Hendrix and Miss Schopenhauer shouldn't—oh, and the cleaners and gardeners too!—shouldn't have to put up with that kind of thing. I won't allow it."

There was a pause that I took for an invitation to speak, but I remained mute, mulling over the situation as it was described to me.

"So, Lancaster," said Amelia, "do you have any questions?"

"I do not, ma'am."

"We're horrified that you were bitten," said Amelia.

"And even more horrified that Lucifer told you to 'let it go,'" Dudley added with visible distress.

I found myself bristling slightly. "I hope Mr. Hendrix hasn't been speaking out of turn."

It was Amelia's turn to bristle. "If Liam decided that he ought to say something to us, especially about something as serious as this, it would not be out of turn, Lancaster."

"I beg your pardon."

"Besides," interjected Dudley, "it wasn't Liam. Lucifer told us himself that he'd instructed you to let the whole thing go. Or not to worry about it. Something like that."

"Yes sir."

"Amy gave him a piece of her mind," said Dudley. "When Lucifer said he'd told you to let it go, I thought she was going to throw him out a window."

"I am sure—"

"That's everything," said Amelia. "Thank you, Lancaster."

"Very good," I said. I nodded and took my leave.

I found Paige washing dishes. I crossed the room and sat on her counter. She watched me in surprise.

"Mr. Lancaster?"

"Miss Schopenhauer."

"Do you want tea?"

I shook my head. "Thank you, no."

"Are you feeling alright?"

I shook my head. The knowledge that Amelia was angry with me left me feeling sick to my stomach.

Paige towelled off her densely freckled forearms and filled a litre container with water. "Here." Normally I couldn't come into this kitchen without being teased mercilessly, but now Paige was watching my face with an expression of sincere concern.

"Thank you," I said.

She stood in front of me, struggling to untie her apron. "I haven't wiped down that counter yet," she said apologetically.

"Doesn't matter."

"Doesn't it? I've never known anyone so fussy about his clothes."

"I couldn't care less about my clothes."

"Really? You're always fixing them and straightening them and—"

"Mrs. Peterkin is angry with me."

"Oh?"

"Why?"

"Are you asking me why she's angry with you?"

I put the water down on the counter and slid to the floor. I winced as the edge of the counter rubbed against the bruise on my thigh. I sniffed angrily and made for the back door.

"Where are you going?" Paige asked, her voice rising slightly.

"I need air."

I stepped onto the lawn, closed my eyes, and took a long, deep breath. I could hear the cook's footsteps pursuing me.

"Mr. Lancaster." Paige caught me by the elbow. "Hey."

"I'm sorry, Miss Schopenhauer. It's just that I'm struggling to know how best to serve the Peterkins right now."

"I know."

"And I'm not fussy about my clothes."

"Oh, Mr. Lancaster," she said kindly, patting my arm. "Yes, you are. You're literally straightening your tie right now."

I quickly put my hands in my coat pockets. "Do you know who taught me how to tie a tie?"

"I honestly assumed you were born wearing one."

"Mr. Pappas. He taught me how to run room service as soon as I was big enough. He taught me how to tie a tie and shine shoes. When I was older, he showed me how to shave."

"Sounds like a great boss."

"I don't think he was."

"Oh."

"But he permitted me to sleep in the basement of his hotel when I was nine."

"Mr. Lancaster—"

"Why is Mrs. Peterkin mad at me?"

Paige sighed. "It's not you. She just feels helpless. She's obsessed with being the bigger woman, but her life is being tugged up by the roots and she kind of wants to scream. She had all those awful people in the house this weekend because Dudley is being an idiot, and now she feels like you were trying to hide the whole incident with the dog bite from her. She just feels ganged up on."

"Thank you, Miss Schopenhauer."

Hoffman caught me as I was doing my rounds outside that evening.

"Hey! Lancaster!"

"Good evening, Mr. Hoffman." I picked up a small branch that had fallen from one of the oak trees and tossed it into the mulch under a hedge. "I was given to understand that you had already retired for the evening."

"I did," said Hoffman, "but then I had gas. I thought I'd walk it off."

I suppressed a grimace.

"Heard that feral rat in there bit you."

"Yes," I said.

Hoffman drew near and kicked at a shrub without malice. "But my idiot son-in-law isn't throwing them out," he observed.

I continued with my inspection of the grounds. Hoffman followed me closely, growling hostilities and farting constantly.

* * *

The next couple of days passed without incident.

After some debate, Hieronymus was sent away to a canine behaviour school where he was to remain for several months. It was the sincere hope of every person in the household that the badger spawn would be returned with civil manners and orderly habits.

Lucian spent all of Wednesday and Thursday in his studio, making good on his end of the patronage by sketching ideas for ghastly canvases. It was always evident when he was hard at work, because he played podcasts on a Bluetooth speaker. The sounds of unqualified voices pretentiously judging society for its ills wafted through the open window of the studio to pollute the grounds with rhetorical smog.

Kandyss was also hard at work. Paige, who had made the personal decision to follow Kandy Kane on Instagram, took great delight in showing me pictures and videos of the influencer demonstrating the use of a facewash or hand cream.

The Peterkins were both quite busy with work. Neither spoke to me beyond what was necessary.

I don't believe they were any more conversational with one another.

Even if there was tension in the air, most of the household enjoyed some peace for those two days. This was not true of Patrick Hoffman. That gentleman was immovable in his horror of the Tremblays. He was in a perpetual state of complete shock and disgust, sickened by the knowledge that the Tremblays still inhabited the East Wing. It was with pure, unaffected dismay that he observed Kandyss Tremblay jogging down Harper's Lane or overheard Lucian Tremblay's podcasts during our evening drink in the garden.

On Thursday evening, when the Tremblays were making themselves drinks in the gazebo where Hoffman and I often set up bottle and glasses, the elderly gentleman and I retreated to a picturesque corner of the grounds where, concealed behind a rose garden, we made use of a cast-iron table and chairs.

"It's too bad," said Hoffman, attempting to make himself a martini, "that they sent away the dog." He poured indiscriminately, and behold, some gin fell among the digestives, some fell upon the table, and some fell into his glass.

"Oh?" I moved my feet hastily as gin rained down from the patterned tabletop to the grass below.

"If it had mauled the kid, even Dudley would see that these people are a menace."

"Such a scenario, however idyllic to the present imagination, would come at some personal cost to Mr. Hendrix."

"If you're going to talk like a prick, don't talk at all," snapped Hoffman. He used his fingers to fish several olives out of the small jar I had stolen from Paige's kitchen and dropped them into his drink. He pulled at the gin with an unhappy expression and smacked his lips. He took the olive jar and tipped some of its brine into his glass. A second experimental sip seemed to bring more satisfaction, and he slouched contentedly into his chair. "You know what I mean," he said. "At least a bite or two would give them all something to really fight about."

I selected a digestive that looked dry and turned it over in my hands thoughtfully. "Perhaps you're right," I said.

* * *

On Friday, the artist sat before a set of preliminary sketches and a coloured compositional mock-up. He basked in the effect of the different images for almost an hour, occasionally darting forward to accentuate some feature or correct another.

When Liam appeared to announce that lunch things were present in the dining room, Lucian waved him in.

"What do you think?" asked the artist, positioning the underbutler toward the back of the studio where he could observe sketches and canvas alike to maximum advantage.

"And what did you say?" asked Paige.

"I didn't know what to say," said Liam, his mouth full of sandwich. "I honestly didn't know what I was looking at. There weren't a lot of details."

"But surely you said something," I pressed.

Liam nodded, but he was obliged to swallow before speaking. "Yeah," he said. "I asked him to explain his vision to me."

"Well done," I said.

"So he just goes off talking about it, and by the time he had finished explaining, he wasn't interested in my opinion anymore. He was that fired up."

"Smart boy," said Paige admiringly.

That was all on Friday. To celebrate his readiness to actually start a painting, Lucian and Kandyss decided to spend a weekend away. They drove off in search of a town large enough to paint red, where they doubtless planned to abuse restaurant and casino staff until their return on Sunday evening.

"Seems a little premature for debauchery," said Amelia dryly when Dudley told her of the Tremblays' weekend plans. "I generally open a bottle after I finish a book. Not when I decide what I'm going to write."

"He told me that he's starting the painting on Monday," said Dudley.

"Did he tell you anything about this foetal masterpiece?"

"He says it has to do with hypocrisy of some kind."

"Oh good."

(Monday, April 25)

There were two Tremblay-related items listed in my logbook for the last Monday of April. Firstly, Lucian Tremblay began work on the first painting of his patronage.

Secondly, Kandyss Tremblay asked to see me.

I entered the East Wing with something resembling trepidation. I was surprised to find Kandyss dressed in a tan pantsuit with shoulder pads. She sat at the head of the white dining table, her hands folded in front of her. She gazed down the length of that immaculate surface at its one ornament—the table of Roman Law that she had been gifted by Lucian.

"Mrs. Tremblay?"

She didn't look up at my salutation but mumbled an acknowledgment of my presence. She continued to stare at the sheet of stone in its glistening frame of brass. Perhaps it was the dated business attire and perhaps it was a trick of the lighting, but for a moment she looked like a young Hillary Clinton. It was an oddly inappropriate comparison, and I blinked it away hastily.

"Mr. Hendrix gave me to understand that you wanted to see me," I said.

"Yes."

Apparently satisfied with the conversation's progress, my summoner allowed silence to fall once more. I joined her in studying the tablet. I cannot pretend to know why Amelia Peterkin believed it to be a fraud. It looked quite ancient to my ill-informed eyes. I have always admired the beautiful, uniform curves of lettering carved into stone. It always makes me wonder how it was achieved with hammers and chisels.

Mrs. Tremblay began to speak, and her voice was, as always, oddly childish.

"I want my bathroom cleaned more regularly," she meowed. "When I say *my bathroom,* I mean the one in the hall on the second floor. The one with the gable window. It's the one I use most regularly."

I was a little surprised to hear this. The East Wing boasted six full bathrooms, one of which adjoined the Tremblays' bedroom. It was not clear why Kandyss would be using the gabled bathroom, which was not located near any rooms in regular use.

"You use that one more often than your en suite?" I know that it was not a proper question, now that I reflect on it, but I was genuinely puzzled.

"The en suite doesn't have windows. The one with the gable is the only south-facing bathroom in the place. It has wonderful natural light."

"I see."

"I need good lighting for my work."

"Just as you say."

"But I want the room cleaned more often. It's only cleaned three days a week. I want it tidied on the in-between days as well."

I resisted the urge to point out that the Peterkins were generally able to keep things tidy enough between visits from the maids. Instead, I performed a docile nod. "I will instruct Mr. Hendrix to clean that bathroom on the off days going forward," I said.

"Thanks."

Kandyss went back to studying the artifact in the table's centre as if to signal the conversation's conclusion.

I fished for my dismissal. "Was there anything more that you needed, Mrs. Tremblay?"

She shook her head but didn't speak or look in my direction.

I ducked my head and turned to leave.

"Lancaster." The voice was still that of Kandyss, but it was suddenly lower. It was almost hoarse.

I bit my tongue and turned back. "Ma'am."

"Why did Lucy give this thing to me?"

I glanced at the tablet uneasily. "The stone, Mrs. Tremblay?"

She nodded. Perhaps it was the lighting again, but for a moment I thought she was looking very flushed.

"I am sure it was meant as a token of Mr. Tremblay's affection for you, ma'am." I have rarely issued more brazen a lie.

"No, it's not," she snapped. I could think of no reply, but she wasn't waiting for one. "I don't even know what it is," she said angrily. "I even read that stupid piece of paper it came with again, and I still couldn't really explain it to anybody. I've never cared about history."

"Perhaps it was a miscalculation," I said carefully, "but well-meant nonetheless."

"Bull," she said.

"If you say so," I said. This was not my kind of conversation.

"Do you know what it's like to be married to a man who wishes you were smarter or more sophisticated?"

"Not from experience."

"You know, my mother told me that men only want One Thing. My aunt said so too. When I was twenty and all my male friends were twenty, it seemed like it was true."

I wanted to leave. In fact, I almost asked permission to do just that. However, there was something fascinating about hearing Kandyss speak coherently. As the moment's impropriety impressed itself on me, I stood a little straighter and raised my chin, but I did not leave.

"You know who knows all about this thing?" Kandyss pointed at the tablet. "Amy. Your boss. Just look at her. I mean... I know Lucy does."

"Perhaps," I said quickly, "I should return to my other—"

Kandyss's voice resumed its high pitch as if this would ensure my staying a little longer. "I just keep looking at it, you know, and asking myself: *Why?* Why would he give me a gift that would be so much better for Amy? Do you think he wants me to become like Amy? Do you think he wanted Amy to see that he's, like, a smartass for getting something like this? Like, 'Look at me. I appreciate finer things. Not like my idiot bimbo wife.'"

I opened my mouth and shut it again.

"You can say it," said Kandyss. "You don't have to be all butlery."

"I'm sure that it would not be my place to comment on any of the speculations you propose," I said. "I will merely repeat that I think the gift was most likely a sincere token of his affection."

"Then you're not very smart," said Kandyss nastily. "I think he gave it to me because he wants more than just the One Thing. He wants me to be more. More like Amy."

"Please forgive me," I said. "I really must excuse myself."

"So I've got to clean the bathrooms now?" There was nothing mutinous in Liam's question, but I could tell that he was displeased.

"Only the one," I said, "and only on Tuesdays, Thursdays, and Saturdays."

"It's a bit of an ask, isn't it?"

"It is."

"You're not going to complain to the Peterkins about it?"

"No. It is an unusual request, but far from outrageous. I once held my post in a house where I was required to change a capuchin monkey's diapers. This is hardly so onerous a duty, I assure you. Besides, you don't have to deep clean it, you know. Just wipe it down. Empty the trash. Freshen it up a bit."

The underbutler nodded sullenly. "Very good," he said.

I was proud of him. "Tell you what," I said. "I'll do it for you on Tuesdays."

"Oh, you don't have to do that."

"Nonsense," I said firmly. "I insist."

It rained that evening, so Mr. Hoffman and I took our drinks into the kitchen of the warden's cottage and played gin rummy. The drumming of rain on the windows and shingles very nearly drowned out the sound of Liam playing a video game in his room. The kettle whistled softly.

"Be a good man and pour the grog," said Hoffman.

I rose and prepared two mugs of rum and hot water. I sliced a wheel of lemon into each and brought them back to the table.

"So now the kid has to clean her toilet," said Hoffman. He held his mug under his nose and inhaled deeply as if the vapours might warm his brain.

"He does," I said, collecting my hand and inspecting the cards.

"It's your turn."

I drew a card. "I offered to clean it on Tuesdays." I pulled a knave out of my deadwood and reached for the discard pile, rapping my knuckles on the tabletop as I did so.

Hoffman swore and threw down his cards. Thirty-four deadwood. "I could have knocked earlier, Lancaster, but then I thought I might go for gin. Idiot."

I opened my phone and added the score to our scoresheet in my note-taking app. "Such is the nature of the game we're playing, Mr. Hoffman. One must exercise patience, but one must also maintain a sense of urgency."

Hoffman took a long swig of his grog as I began to shuffle the deck. "Don't lecture me," he growled with a cough. "Just mind how you play your own hand."

* * *

Over the days and weeks that followed, Lucian Tremblay made steady progress on The Painting. To his credit, he spent most of every day in the studio. His podcasts and music continued to seep out of the window while the man busied himself with the business of creating art.

The Peterkins were forbidden to see the work in progress, with the promise of an eventual reveal ceremony. This was a poetic notion, but it also put a peculiar strain on the artist, as the canvas over which he laboured became more and more symbolic. It ceased to be just another painting to add to his catalogue. Instead, it was his justification. The patronage of Dudley Peterkin could not be spent in the production of mediocrity. This was Lucian's moment to show just how brilliant he could be if someone would only pay his way and leave him to focus entirely on his craft.

Fortunately for Paige and me, the ban that prevented the Peterkins from seeing the painting did nothing to stop Liam from coming and going.

"I don't think it's my style," said Paige.

"Are all these things bodies?" I asked, pointing to the small screen of Liam's phone.

"Yes! It's like... a giant heap of bodies. Everyone is mad at the person standing on their shoulders, but they're also standing on somebody else's."

"Bit morbid," said Paige.

"I think I kinda get it," said Liam. "I keep thinking about it, and it's kind of starting to make sense."

"Mir, Zemlya, i Khleb!" I said without feeling.

(Tuesday, May 3)

Just over a week after he began the work, Lucian announced that he had applied the final touches to The Painting. This announcement was made over lunch in the gazebo. The Peterkins and Tremblays were seated precisely as they had been on that fateful day when the latter first came to discuss the patronage with the Peterkins. The only addition was Mr. Hoffman, who was seated at the foot of the table.

"The painting is finished already?" said Amelia, impressed. "That was so fast!"

Mrs. Peterkin was in fine spirits. She had spent much of the past week giving guest lectures and visiting with her brother and his family. That reprieve from the antics of Harper's Lane seemed to have done her good.

"Not if you include the weeks of conception and preparation that took place before ever I dipped my brush," said Lucian.

"Besides," said Kandyss brightly, "it's a tiny canvas."

Lucian looked at her sharply. "It's not about the size," he snapped. "It's about the story it tells."

"Haha!" snorted Hoffman.

Liam and I made eye contact but remained dutifully expressionless.

"Dad!" Amelia chided.

"So can we see it today?" Dudley asked.

Lucian was in the act of raising a spoonful of soup to his mouth. He shook his head and then inserted the spoon. There was a brief lull in the conversation as he savoured and swallowed before responding to Dudley's question. "No," he said. "The paint I put on this morning needs a chance to dry before I show it. In truth," he said, leaning back with the air of a lecturer, "I would prefer to keep it drying for a few weeks and then show it after I've had a chance to apply some varnish. But." Here he winked at Dudley. "I think my patron has been patient enough."

"So," said Dudley, "tomorrow then?"

Lucian nodded grudgingly. "Come by before lunch and I'll give you a little show. I'll prop up a few of my other canvases that you haven't seen. Might interest you as well," he said, looking at Amelia.

"I wouldn't miss it for the world," said Amelia agreeably. "I've been so curious to see what's going on in that studio of yours!"

Kandyss stood up quite suddenly. "Thank you for lunch," she said sweetly. "Sorry for running, but I have a bunch of work that needs doing this afternoon."

"Do you?" asked Lucian in a tone of amazement.

"I do."

"Thank you for making time to have lunch with us," said Dudley cordially.

"Yes," agreed Amelia. "It's always a pleasure."

Kandyss simpered and tripped off toward the house.

"Don't work too hard, Kandyss!" Lucian called after her. He chuckled and waded once more into his soup.

Amelia opened her mouth and closed it a couple of times. I could tell she was looking for just the right words. I couldn't imagine what they might be. "Lucifer," she said at last, "I was so impressed by that gift you gave Kandyss a few weeks ago."

"Ah!" said Lucian, swallowing hastily. He smiled eagerly at this change of topic. "I thought you might be."

"Right," said Dudley. "Though maybe *surprised* is a better word than *impressed.*"

"Yes," said Amelia.

"Why is that?" asked Lucian.

"It's such an unusual piece!" said Amelia diplomatically. "There are some people out there who would definitely question some of the claims made about it."

"Really." This appeared unthinkable to Lucian. His smile had faded, but not entirely. It seemed to be gradually morphing into his habitual sneer.

"I have a friend," said Amelia. "She's a really good friend, and this kind of thing is right up her alley. I was talking to her about something else yesterday and mentioned your tablet. She said she'd be happy to look it over for you."

"I'll bet she would."

"And the thing is," said Amelia, "if there's anything inaccurate about what you were told, you might be able to get some money back, depending on where you got it. If it *is* everything you were told, then you'll have extra confirmation that what you have is a very special piece indeed."

Lucian laughed. "A win-win," he said.

"I would think so," said Dudley. I could tell that my employer wasn't happy with the way this conversation was going. His eyes were narrowed ever so slightly, and he had the look of a guard dog trying to decide if there was a threat present.

"I think it's fine," said Lucian. "I know what we have. I checked it myself."

"Sure," said Amelia hurriedly. "Absolutely. I didn't mean to question your judgement, obviously, and there's no pressure. I just thought I'd let you know about my friend. If you want to leave it, that's totally fine. If you want to have it looked at again by an extra set of eyes, I can put you in touch."

"So gracious," said Lucian coldly, "as always."

"Are you being sarcastic?" Dudley asked abruptly.

It wasn't like Dudley Peterkin to look for conflict, but I was glad to hear him cut in. The condescending tone Lucian was using to address Amelia was inspiring me with warlike thoughts. It would have been entirely unnatural if her own husband had been indifferent to it.

"Oh, I'm sure he's not," said Amelia. Her tone was less friendly than her words.

"Eh," drawled Lucian, preparing to become long-winded. "Here's the thing. You say I could either get money back or be reassured that the tablet is what I think it is."

"Right," said Amelia.

"But I can imagine a third option. I have something rare. The only one of its kind. You take it to your friend. She's your friend! You're friends. So naturally she does you a favour and tells me that it's a piece of garage sale trash. I *maybe* get some money back from the auction house, and you kindly offer to make it up to me by buying the tablet for a few bucks. Now I have most of my money back. No complaints. But you? You have a priceless, incredibly rare piece that you just couldn't let by. The best part (and you'll have to tell all your friends) is that you got it for a few bucks from a peasant who didn't know what he had."

Liam and I looked at one another in shared horror. We should have left moments earlier. Now, with a quarrel breaking out, it would seem dramatic for the staff to scatter. We were like deer in headlights.

"Okay," said Dudley.

"Oh, my goodness!" cried Amelia.

"That's completely uncalled for," said Dudley, rising to his feet, his knuckles pressed into the table's surface. He hadn't yet raised his voice, but his face was a dangerous shade of red.

"Dudley, sit." Amelia pulled at his arm.

"I'm just calling it like I see it," said Lucian, throwing up his hands in an exaggerated expression of helplessness.

"Get your eyes checked!" snapped Dudley. "You don't know the first thing about antiquities, and Amy is just trying to make sure you don't get ripped off!"

"Dudley," said Amelia in an even tone, "I think I've got this."

Dudley sat, bristling.

"Mr. Tremblay," said Amelia in a soft, unruffled voice, "if you do not want your stone looked at, that's fine. Personally, I think you've been lied to. So even if I were such a mean, desperate person as you describe, I would never make any effort whatsoever to add that mislabelled piece of granite to my collection. If you wish to keep it, that's your own business. If you want to have it inspected, you'll have to find an expert of your own. As it is, I am no longer interested in connecting you with my friend."

"Thanks for lunch," said Lucian, rising. He grinned insolently at his hosts and slouched off toward the house. No words were spoken until the inelegant figure had passed from view.

"What a jerk!" cried Dudley. "I'd like to have given him a piece of my mind!"

"Dudley," said Amelia quietly, "I'm done. I'm just..." She sat back and shook her head, her arms folded across her chest. Her eyes wandered over the gardens. She looked sad and thoughtful as she inspected those sacred surroundings. "I'm done."

"What do you mean?"

"I'm just done." She stood and set off toward the kitchen door.

Dudley slouched and looked simultaneously enraged and heartbroken. Quite suddenly, he remembered that he was not alone. With a sigh, he awkwardly shuffled into a straighter posture in his seat. "Lancaster."

"Sir."

"Sorry about that."

"Not at all, sir."

"Thank you for the lunch service. Tell Paige that it was delicious."

"I will."

"Thank you too, Liam."

Liam nodded. "My pleasure, sir."

"Why don't you go inside for a few minutes?"

"Yes sir."

Together, my employer and I watched the young man's back until he was out of earshot.

"Crap!" said Dudley. "Crap, crap, crap." He rested his face against his clenched fist, biting his knuckles. "Lancaster?"

"Sir?"

Dudley threw his arms wide. "What am I supposed to do now?"

"I'm sure it wouldn't be my place to say."

"Lancaster!"

"I am not a married man, Mr. Peterkin."

Dudley leapt to his feet and shoved the table. Three glasses fell. Water ran to the floor of the gazebo in loud little waterfalls. "You're a human! Help me out! Do I shake him by the throat and tell him to apologise to Amy? Is that the thing to do?"

I bit my pursed lips.

"Or maybe I go and try to talk her down? Or maybe give her a minute? What do you think she meant when she said she's done?"

"I really can't say."

"What is this?" Dudley circled the table as if about to head into the house but kept his gaze on me. He grabbed the back of one of the chairs and glared at me. "You're just going to stand there and watch my house come to bits? You don't care? You little..."

He stopped himself, making a great effort to calm down. With a trembling hand he picked up one of the fallen water glasses, as if preparing to tidy up the disheveled table. He was struck by another wave of distress and looked up at me with an ugly expression. "So you're just going to keep your distance and stay professional and not even try to help? You know what? You know what?"

I waited to hear what, but Dudley never finished that particular thought. Instead, he flung the glass against the sill of the gazebo, shattering it into a thousand pieces that sparkled and sang as they fell about us.

“Sir—” I began to speak, but Dudley held up a hand.

“Forget it,” he said. He turned, and like everyone else, started stalking away toward the house.

I stood perfectly still for several seconds, collecting myself. I polished my glasses. I tugged on my waistcoat. I straightened my cuffs. I polished my glasses again, breathing long, deliberate breaths. I looked out across the rich, abundant gardens, as Amelia had done. Not so long ago, this home had inhabited a bubble. That bubble had been the Peterkins’ means of preserving their peace and privacy. It had been mine to maintain. It still was.

Where Lucian spent the rest of his afternoon is anybody’s guess.

Kandyss’s afternoon, on the other hand, could have been recreated to the minute by her activity on social media. She responded to comments, posted on three platforms, and engaged with other influencers’ content. Then she went back, did another sweep of comments, and stalked the accounts of a handful of new followers.

After dinner, Lucian told Liam that he was going to go into town and get into trouble. He took a taxi instead of driving, which was probably a decent example of foresight.

Kandyss had different evening plans. As her husband set out, she prepared to film a video in her bathroom. She had been sent fizzy bath bombs by a sponsor, and according to one of her Instagram stories that afternoon, she was unreservedly excited about the opportunity to test them.

I naturally knew nothing of these plans. Mr. Hoffman and I were busy searching the kitchen for oranges (in the hopes of making negronis) when my phone began to vibrate. According to the caller ID, it was Liam.

"Excuse me, Mr. Hoffman," I said. I closed the stand-up and moved over to the undercounter fridge, answering the phone as I went. "Mr. Hendrix?"

"Mr. Lancaster, I've just received a call from Mrs. Tremblay. She says she's made a mess in one of the bathrooms. She needs help cleaning it up."

I removed an orange from under the counter and looked at it wistfully. "I'll be right there."

When Liam and I arrived on the second floor of the East Wing, Kandyss had already lost the battle. The bath was running unencumbered, and a steady sheet of water poured over its edge onto the tile floor. Towels, plastic bottles, and several brightly coloured luffas floated and spun in the diluvian hellscape. Directly in the centre of the scene was a gigantic duvet, apparently brought from one of the bedrooms to serve as a bigger and better towel. On this island of sodden white bedding was perched Kandyss herself. She was wearing a red bathrobe and looked like a cherry on a vanilla sundae, if that sundae had been dropped into a sewer.

The cherry had apparently given up. She looked up as we entered, her face streaked with dark rivulets of tears and mascara. "I'm sorry," she whispered.

Liam and I darted at once for the tub.

"Why isn't it draining?" I asked Kandyss.

"I don't know!"

"Where's the handle for the controls?" Liam shouted upon discovering that the object in question was missing.

"It fell off!" croaked Kandyss. "I couldn't stop the water!"

I saw the circular control for the shower lying at the bottom of the tub and sighed deeply. This bath was not, sadly, one of the old-fashioned oval tubs that one pictures by default upon hearing the term "bath." Instead, this was one of those modern luxury tubs that seemed to be inspired by the dimensions and topography of a skateboard park. It was set into the floor so that to reach the bottom, one had to descend a small flight of three steps.

Liam uttered an involuntary exclamation.

"Mr. Hendrix," I said with another sigh, "please mind your language and my coat."

The water was surprisingly hot, and I winced as I descended the steps. As I entered the water, an extra cascade leapt out of the tub to the bathroom floor, emphasising the urgency of the situation. Submerged almost to the seat of my trousers, I waded awkwardly to where the control handle lay and plunged my arm in after it.

"I already tried putting it back on!" Kandyss wailed. "It won't go!"

Nevertheless, I waded to the panel where the control should have gone and tried to reattach it. There were touchscreen options, but they only controlled temperature, lighting, and water agitation. The flow was entirely dependent upon the saucer-shaped piece of metal in my hands. I looked into the recess where the control should fit and saw nothing for it to attach to.

"Mr. Hendrix!" I cried. "Go down to the utility room and shut off the water for this bathroom. It'll be one of the pairs of taps on the east wall. They should be marked!"

Liam, as previously mentioned, was an excellent runner. Off he shot, my coat still draped over his arm.

As we waited for the water to be disconnected, I continued in my vain effort to get the control back on its moorings. As I was in the midst of this struggle, I felt my foot brush against something and saw a small collection of metal and plastic parts scattered around the floor of the tub. This control was not going to be of any use tonight.

Liam must have found the water line, as the flow was suddenly cut off.

"Well," I said, tossing the disc back into the tub, "that's that."

"I didn't do this!" Kandyss announced. "The water wouldn't drain, and the thing fell off. What was I supposed to do?"

"I'm sure I don't know." I waded over to the drain. It was a discrete orifice, a mere rectangular slot located under a sculpted seat. I bent down and felt around the opening of the drain, but there was nothing there. I took a deep breath and got down on my knees so that I could reach in further. I could feel a very weak current indicating that some water was draining, but not nearly as fast as it had been entering the tub. Then my fingers found fabric. I pulled and twisted at the fabric until it came away from the drain. As I withdrew my hand, I could feel the drain's proper current restored.

I stood and tried to blink water from my eyes. I felt a towel thrust into my free hand, and with this I was able to dry my face. "Thank you, Mr. Hendrix," I said, passing the towel back to the underbutler. I looked at the piece of fabric I had removed from the drain and saw that it was a bright pink bathrobe of delicate construction.

"Oh!" said Kandyss faintly. "That's mine."

"Let's get this mess cleaned up," I said to Liam.

He nodded. "I'll go get more towels," he said.

"And I'll go get the wet vacuum." I turned to the cherry, who still had not left her duvet sundae. "Mrs. Tremblay, we will be just a minute in returning."

Kandyss nodded numbly. We left her there, still seated pathetically in a sea of her own making, clutching her bathrobe unhappily.

When we returned, the cherry had vanished.

"Probably just as well," said Liam, grimly dropping a couple of plastic tubs near the door and separating them. "It wouldn't be any easier with her sitting there."

I nodded my agreement and plugged in the vacuum. It roared like a small airplane, and I began removing the majority of the water from the floor. It was due to the noise of the wet vacuum and our focus on our work that we didn't hear Kandyss return. I only realised that we were not alone when I saw her reflection in one of the bathroom mirrors. I started and turned.

For the first time since I'd met her, Kandyss was dressed sensibly. She wore jeans and a loose T-shirt. Her hair was tied back, and though her face was still stained by her weeping from earlier, she seemed to have recovered some composure. She was looking at me expectantly.

I turned off the vacuum. "Mrs. Tremblay?"

"How can I help?" she asked. It was a game display, and I almost felt guilty.

"Oh Mrs. Tremblay," I said, "Mr. Hendrix and I can take care of this. I'm only sorry you had such a terrible experience this evening."

Kandyss ignored me and joined Liam, who was in the process of gathering the waterlogged duvet into one of the two plastic bins. Liam took an armful of dry towels out of the other bin and stacked them on the counter. Kandyss took the top towel and started drying the floor in the hallway. I thought about discouraging her further involvement. It would have been more appropriate if Mr. Hendrix and I took care of this disaster alone. Instead, however, I turned the vacuum back on and returned to the task at hand.

(Wednesday, May 4)

I told the Peterkins about the previous night's adventures while serving them breakfast the next morning.

"You could've told us that was going on," said Dudley. He was wearing another one of those blinding shirts he had picked up in New York.

"I should not have liked to disturb you unduly," I replied. This was true. Since the Tremblays had moved in, a chill cloud had been slowly developing over and about and between the

Peterkins. This cloud had grown significantly since the previous day's lunch. I still wasn't sure what Amelia had meant by "I'm done," but I did know that the air over the breakfast table was positively icy. I reflected that this atmosphere was in no way helped by the presence of Dudley's shirt.

"It is your job to tell us these things," said Amelia.

"That is why I mention it now," I said, choosing my words with care. "There was no need at the time. Mr. Hendrix and I were more than able to clean things up without bothering you. I should also mention that Mrs. Tremblay was kind enough to assist us."

"And Mr. Tremblay?" asked Amelia.

"Mr. Tremblay was still out when we finished."

"Wonder when he got back," muttered Dudley darkly. To me he said, "Thank you for taking care of that, Lancaster. Is the bathroom out of commission?"

"It is at present," I said. "The water will have to remain off until the bath can be repaired. A serviceman will be coming to take a look at it either later today or early tomorrow."

"You're so efficient," said Amelia. She gave me a smile, but I noticed that her eyes were tired and dull. She had clearly been crying recently. As if aware of my observations, she looked away sharply. "Anyway, I'm sure the Tremblays will be able to make do with their other bathrooms for now."

Hoffman entered. He was late, which was usual, but in excellent spirits, which was less usual. "What have I missed?" he asked, taking his regular seat next to his daughter. "Where's my coffee? Talking about the Tremblays, huh? Are you still going over there to look at his awful painting today?"

Dudley sighed. "I suppose so."

"Are you?" Amelia looked at him sharply.

"Do you think he'll be expecting us to come?"

"Do you expect me to?"

Dudley missed a beat and choked out an awkward: "Oh. Hmm."

Amelia sighed. "It's fine. No, Lancaster," she said, stopping me as I was making for the door. "It's fine. We're fine. I can be the bigger person, Dudley." She looked at Dudley significantly.

Dudley looked back significantly.

Hoffman looked at me significantly.

I examined the ceiling but found there nothing of significance.

Lucian didn't rise until after eleven, and the first thing he remembered was that he had promised to give the Peterkins a show of his art that morning. He called Dudley and asked if they were free to come over in five minutes.

Immediately after getting off the phone with Dudley, Lucian called Liam and asked if he could bring over some champagne and maybe something to eat. I took care of the champagne and left Liam to talk Paige into preparing a cold board of some kind.

I arrived in the East Wing at the same time as the Peterkins. I poured four flutes of Bollinger and offered them to those present.

Lucian seized the nearest glass like one dehydrated (which he probably was) and downed half of it in a greedy gulp. "None too soon," he gasped.

I smiled and presented the flutes to the others.

"No, thank you," said Amelia.

"I'm sure you're curious!" said Lucian, positioning himself in front of the door to his studio. Apparently, a speech was required. "I'm sure you're wondering what you'll find in here. Beauty? Joy? Despair? Guilt? Inspiration? I'll admit that I'm curious what you'll find in here as well. That's art, isn't it? How can I know what sentiment will burst into flower in each of you as you see the fruit of my labours? I'm also curious because I haven't seen the painting since the finishing touches I applied yesterday have had a chance to dry." This last comment was delivered ruefully, and it was clearly supposed to be droll.

Dudley smiled obligingly. Amelia tilted her head back and looked pensive.

"Curious is right," said Dudley cheerfully.

"Well then. I'll shut up and let you enter into the all-telling dialogue that art seeks to hold with its beholder." The studio had a pocket door, and with the attitude of one pulling back a curtain, Lucian slid the door aside and waved his audience in.

Reactions were immediate.

"Shoot," said Dudley.

Kandyss made a strangled groan.

I stiffened.

At first, Lucian seemed delighted by the expressions of shock and dismay on the faces before him. This, apparently, was how he had hoped to see people respond to The Painting. He took a long sip of his champagne and nodded, satisfied.

"I'm so sorry," murmured Kandyss.

Lucian was more surprised at these words and turned to inspect his studio. Upon seeing it, he joined the rest of the party in expressing horror. He howled like a wounded animal and dropped to his knees. He stammered out a pained obscenity.

The floor of the studio was covered in water. Several of the canvases that had been leaning against the room's walls had been knocked down and washed about. One, an unusually large canvas, lay face down in the flood, the water around its edges running with paint. A small stream of water gushed out into the hallway where we stood.

Dudley and Amelia looked at each other and then at me.

Amelia pointed at the ceiling. She silently mouthed the words, *"Was it that bathroom?"*

I nodded.

Dudley stepped forward to assess the damage. "Hey now," he said, patting Lucian on the shoulder. "Let's take a look. I'm sure it's not all that bad."

It was most certainly all that bad.

Of the forty-some canvases Lucian had put in the studio, only eleven had been left untouched by the water. For most of those affected, only one edge showed water damage, and in those cases it was usually quite minimal. Several canvases, however, were utterly ruined.

As it happened, the piece that had been the subject of that morning's showing was one of those that had remained untouched. Its position on the easel toward the middle of the room had preserved it entirely.

"Oh, I like it," said Dudley, admiring the small canvas from his vantage point in a puddle of paint-mottled water.

"How did this happen?" Lucian howled. He threw his champagne flute into the room, where it shattered on the window.

"Hey now," said Dudley again. He looked at Amelia.

Amelia looked at Kandyss.

Kandyss looked at me.

I looked at Liam, who entered at this point with a board of meats and cheeses.

"Charcuterie?" asked Liam, holding out the board to Amelia. Then he noticed Lucian kneeling on the floor. He took a moment to fully appreciate the situation and then joined Kandyss in looking at me. His eyes were wide.

Lucian tried again, this time more slowly and menacingly. "How. Did. This. Happen."

"Hmm..." said Dudley, making meaningful eye contact with Amelia. "It looks like water came down the walls."

"Does it normally do that?" Lucian asked ferociously, rising to his feet and splashing into the studio. "Does water normally pour out of the ceiling in this room?"

"Maybe a pipe burst," said Amelia.

It suddenly occurred to me that the Peterkins were going to cover for Kandyss.

"Then why isn't it coming down still?" Lucian demanded. He waved about them. "It's not flowing now, is it? If a pipe burst, when was the water shut off?"

"It's automatic," said Dudley.

"What is?"

"Our water system. A dramatic loss of pressure triggers a shutoff valve."

Lucian leaned down and picked up a corner of the large canvas that was floating, corpse-like, on its face. He inspected it for a moment before letting it fall back to the floor. He looked around him, his face twisted in an expression somewhere between anger and thoughtfulness.

"Lancaster, let's call in one of those water-damage specialists," said Dudley briskly. "They can tidy things up here and maybe recommend a way to dry out some of the... the less affected paintings."

"I'm just thinking," said Lucian. He looked up at the ceiling.

"You know what *I'm* thinking," said Dudley. He pointed to The Painting sitting on its easel. "I'm thinking this is a real winner."

Lucian ignored his patron. "Kandy," he said. He looked from the ceiling to his wife, who appeared very pale. "Kandy, were you using the bathroom up there last night?"

"Yes," Kandyss said.

"And?"

"What?"

"Did you flood my studio?"

A beat passed. Then another. Kandyss looked at me. Then Amelia.

"I don't think so," said Kandyss.

"Oh really," said Lucian viciously. He tore out of the studio and past his wife, making for the stairs. He took the steps two at a bound and quickly vanished from sight.

Dudley turned on me, his eyes wide. “Lancaster?”

“It’s immaculate,” I said.

Dudley nodded and puffed his cheeks as he exhaled a long and expressive sigh.

“Thank you,” whispered Kandyss.

“Except that the controls on the tub are broken,” said Liam.

“Is that obvious?” Amelia asked.

Liam shrugged. “Depends if you look at them or not.”

We heard Lucian throw open the bathroom door. For a couple minutes, silence reigned. Thirty seconds is a long time during a silence. Two minutes felt almost physically painful. Kandyss emptied her champagne glass.

The sounds of Lucian’s footfalls returning were gentler and slower than when he’d left. He descended the stairs with his chin on his chest. “Floor’s dry,” he announced as he met the expectant expressions of the group. “Sorry, Kan. I just thought maybe you’d flooded the bathroom and then... well. Anyway.”

“Lucifer,” said Dudley, “we’re going to get your studio fixed up in no time. Lancaster, make some calls. I want to see people in here before the end of the day.”

“At least my most recent work survived,” said Lucian.

“At least?” Dudley put a friendly hand on the artist’s shoulder. “Lucifer. Lucy. This is the best one so far.”

“Have you even had a chance to take it in?”

“I’m struggling to do anything else.”

Lucian nodded. "They say you're only as good as your last, don't they?"

"They know their stuff."

"Lancaster," said Amelia, "you may go and make arrangements. Liam, just leave that platter on the table there. Come on, Kandyss, let's start pulling these paintings onto the bricks outside. It's a lovely day. I don't know anything about art, but I'm sure that the sooner they dry, the better."

"Mrs. Peterkin," I said, "I'm sure that Liam and I—"

"No," said Amelia sternly. "You have lots to do today as it is. Both of you get out of here. There are four of us. I'm sure we can handle it."

"Absolutely," said Dudley. He put down his champagne and rolled up his sleeves.

As I made my rounds that evening, Mr. Hoffman was generous enough to regale me with a story from his years in the diplomatic service. I generally listened to such Munchausen narratives without interrupting the baron. Tonight, I made an exception.

"Mr. Hoffman," I said, "you say your secretary lost a toe to the cold?"

"That's right. Popped right off while he was walking."

"But hadn't the gentleman in question already lost both his feet to gangrene in the mangrove thickets of Burma?"

Hoffman wagged a reproving finger at me. "I think you mean Myanmar," he said.

"I beg your pardon."

"Not at all. So he was about to throw that toe away, like I was saying, but I stopped him. 'You'll want to keep that,' I said. You know why I said that, Lancaster?"

"Hi! Lancaster?" The childlike voice was recognisable anywhere. I turned and beheld the figure of Kandyss sashaying across the lawn toward us.

"Mrs. Tremblay." I greeted her with a polite nod.

"Protein!" cried Hoffman jubilantly.

Kandyss looked at the elderly gentleman with wide eyes. I wondered briefly what a proper conversation between the two might look like.

"May I help you, Mrs. Tremblay?" I asked.

"You already have," she said. "Thank you so much for last night."

"Oho!" said Hoffman.

"Mr. Hoffman," I said, "would you please excuse me for a moment?" I stepped nearer to the house, and Kandyss followed me closely. Hoffman contented himself with kicking gravel into the flowerbeds.

"Do you have to babysit him?" Kandyss asked, still watching Hoffman.

"I do not."

"I was wondering if my bathroom would be ready to use tomorrow."

"I'm afraid not," I said. "The plumber is ordering a new panel for the bath, and it won't be in for at least ten days."

"Oh," said Kandyss. She pouted.

"I'm afraid you will have to make do with one of your other bathrooms," I said. "If you like, I can update you when we hear—"

"But the windows!" Kandyss moaned. She clutched her head as if the stress of her situation was overwhelming her ability to think. What respect she had earned the night before was quickly being spent. Quite suddenly, she looked up into my eyes with a sugary simper. "Lancaster. Lanny."

I straightened slightly and lifted my chin. My hands dropped to my sides and found the side seams of my trousers.

"Lan-Lan."

"Mrs. Tremblay."

"Are there *no* other bathrooms in this castle with south-facing windows?"

"None in the East Wing, Mrs. Tremblay."

"And?"

I noticed that Hoffman had stopped kicking gravel and was watching us with a penetrating glare. His arms were folded across his chest. I got the sense that he was thinking of the negronis we had been obliged to forgo the night before.

"Mrs. Tremblay, the only two south-facing bathrooms are the one that flooded last night and the one across from Mr. Peterkin's office in the West Wing."

"Aha!"

"The upper floor of the West Wing," I said as firmly as I could, "is devoted to the personal rooms of the Peterkins and to offices. It is not within that part of the home Mr. Peterkin has provided for yourself and Mr. Tremblay. If you wish to use those facilities, I can only recommend that you ask permission of Mr. or Mrs. Peterkin."

"Or you, you Lanky Aster."

"Please, Mrs. Tremblay."

(Saturday, May 7)

Paige and I were having lunch together. We used to enjoy these meals most days. More recently, I had been obliged to share her company with Liam. It was perhaps the only thing I could ever have resented about that promising young man. Liam wasn't in the kitchen during this particular lunch, and I savoured his absence.

"Miss Schopenhauer," I said reverently, "this soup is heavenly. I hesitate to ask what you put in it. I fear that knowing how the magic is performed will somehow rob it of its effect."

"Salt," said Paige.

"Ah."

"So nobody's telling Lucifer how his paintings got wrecked," she said. "You're all just keeping a secret."

"Apparently."

"Including Kandy Kane."

"So far."

"And how do you think that's going to work out?"

"It wasn't my idea," I pointed out. "I'm not one for such a cooperation of deceit. Too many people involved."

"And one of them is that Barbie doll."

"It wasn't my idea," I said again.

"When he *inevitably* finds out, what do you think he'll do? Are people afraid he might mistreat Kandyss?"

I sat away from my soup a little. I had considered that already. "I don't know," I said.

"Why else would they be covering for her?"

"I think it just seemed like the thing to do in the moment."

"Would you be worried about it?"

I took a deep breath. I remembered that odd conversation I'd shared with Kandyss in their dining room, the stone tablet sitting on the table between us. When I spoke, it was slowly and carefully. I wanted to make sure that my words were exact. "I think that man *already* mistreats his wife, Miss Schopenhauer. I don't think he'd ever hit her, you know. Not because he's too good for it, or even too weak for it. I just think he has his own ways of being vicious."

Paige narrowed her eyes. "You've thought about this."

"I have. Anyway. For the time being, Mr. Hendrix says he's calmed right down. Apparently, he was positively cheerful this morning."

"Speak of the devil," said Paige.

Liam entered the kitchen door with a tray from the Tremblays' lunch.

"How is Lucifer?" asked Paige.

"Fine," said Liam, emptying the dirty dishes into the dishwasher. "He says he's going to go for a drive this afternoon." He looked at me. "What are the Peterkins up to today, Mr. Lancaster?"

"I should think they'll be in their offices this afternoon," I said.

"Today?" Liam looked surprised. "It's a Saturday."

"Oh yes," I said. "They've both had their work somewhat disrupted by Tremblays this week. They'll probably spend a few hours at least applying themselves to the grindstone."

"Workaholics," said Liam. He caught my eye. "Sorry," he said. "That's out of turn."

"Yes," I agreed.

I was correct in my belief that Dudley and Amelia would retreat to their offices after lunch. When I went to my own office to place some orders and update my house log, both their doors were open as usual.

"How's Lucy's mood?" Dudley asked.

"Remarkably improved," I said with a reassuring smile.

"Is that you, Lancaster?" Amelia called from her office.

"Lancaster," said Dudley, "I just need to make a couple calls. Could you close that door for me?"

"Uh-oh!" Amelia called. "Don't do it, Lancaster!"

"Do it," said Dudley. "Amy is looking for distractions to help her procrastinate."

"That's not true!" cried Amelia. She was smiling.

I was delighted to see this display of good humour between my employers. It had been too long since I had seen anything like it. This was the first time in days that Amelia hadn't seemed tired and sad.

"How many unread emails did you just tell me you had?" called Dudley.

"Shut up," Amelia groaned.

I closed the door and walked to my office. My door was directly across the hall from Amelia's. I paused in the hall between our doorways and gave her a smile and nod by way of greeting.

"Ugh," said the lady of the house. "Would you mind responding to two hundred emails for me, Lancaster?"

"It would be my pleasure," I said good-humouredly. "I should warn you that my want of expertise might do your reputation a disservice."

Amelia shook her head. "I'm sure you would do an admirable job, Lancaster. But no. This is the penance I must pay for spending my youth on wanton ambition." She waved me away. "Shoo!" she said. "I know you have work of your own to do."

I settled into my office and set to work. A happy half-hour rolled by uneventfully. My window was open, and outside were only the sounds of birds and the distant thrum of a car driving down Harper's Lane. I could faintly hear Dudley's voice rising and falling as he conducted his telephone calls, and the rattle of Amelia's beloved mechanical keyboard indicated that she was attacking her email backlog with vim. These sounds were not distracting to me as I worked.

The sound of someone walking in the hall, however, did make me pause.

I looked up and saw Amelia still focused fully on her work. She was wearing her headphones and was probably listening to music. Dudley was still on the phone in his office.

I heard the door of the bathroom close with a click.

"Oh hell," I said. I sat very still and listened intently. I could hear only the faintest sounds of movement in the bathroom, with which my office shared a wall. No running water, thank goodness.

I was trying to decide what, if anything, I ought to do about the situation when I heard Dudley's door open. He was off his phone call. He came down the hall and peeked in on Amelia. He then turned and looked in at me.

"She's finally started," he said with a wink.

I nodded and opened my mouth to speak. He withdrew and stepped back toward his office.

Amelia had seen her husband and pulled off her headphones. "Dud?" she called.

"Hang on," said Dudley. "I'm just going to use the bathroom."

I rose to my feet, my eyes wide.

"Lancaster?" Amelia was startled by my expression.

Dudley opened the bathroom door.

Much research has been done that seeks to understand the dynamics of emotional memory retention. There is reason to suppose that some combination of emotional impact and incident novelty fosters some of our clearest memories. People know this innately, of course, and there is much talk about flashbulb memories. Where were you when the first COVID-19 lockdowns were announced? What were you doing when you heard about 9/11? Such things stay with a person.

I will always be able to describe, in perfect detail, the moment I realised that Dudley Peterkin was walking in on Kandyss Tremblay in the bathroom.

I made no response to Amelia, and no response was necessary. The sound of Kandyss screaming began the afternoon's revelries without any introduction required.

"Hey now!" cried Dudley.

Amelia and I spilled into the hall at precisely the same moment. We were just in time to watch Dudley reel out of the bathroom, his hand clapped over his eyes. He vanished, backwards, through the open door of his office. A crash told us he had fallen.

Kandyss Tremblay materialised in the hall wearing her cherry-red bathrobe. "I'm so sorry!" she cried. She sprang forward to help Dudley back to his feet.

"Kandyss!" shouted Amelia.

Kandyss straightened and looked at Amelia with a guilty wince. All she could think to say was, "Hi." From where I stood, I observed that under the bathrobe she was wearing a revolting one-piece swimsuit that seemed to be decorated with gold sequins.

Amelia's face, which I was watching closely, was assuming an unusual appearance. It was brightly coloured, and little creases were forming around her nose and forehead. I thought in that moment that this must be how Hera looked on a regular basis.

"What do you think you're doing?" Amelia shouted.

"It's not my fault!" cried Kandyss. She pointed at me, which I resented. Fortunately, Amelia wasn't finished.

"Have you lost your little mind?" roared the lady of the house.

Dudley staggered to his feet. "Hey now," he said.

"I'm sorry?" tried Kandyss, tying her bathrobe closed.

"No!" cried Amelia. This girl was on fire. "Kandyss! What reason can you *possibly* give for being in this hallway at this moment wearing... *that?*"

Kandyss pointed into the bathroom. "The windows are south-facing," she said. She pouted, apparently hoping that her exaggerated moue would help her case. It did not.

"So what?" Amelia took a couple steps toward Kandyss. "It's not your bathroom. You have bathrooms. This is not one of them. This is our bathroom. For our offices. In our wing of the house. You have six bathrooms, Kandyss! You should be in one of those!"

"That's true," said Dudley.

"And why aren't you dressed?" demanded Amelia.

This was a good question. In fact, to my mind, it seemed the most pressing.

"I was going to use the bath," said Kandyss meekly.

"You were going to use the bath." Amelia's voice was suddenly quieter and as cold as ice. "Why do you need south-facing windows to take a bath, Kandyss?"

Dudley and I made eye contact. We recognised in one another's gaze that terrified, perversely excited gleam that enters the heart of a man watching a scene of inevitable violence.

Kandyss made the daring choice to become sulky and pedantic at this point in the conversation. "I wasn't going to *take* a bath," she said, "I was going to *use* it." She reached into the pocket of her bathrobe and produced a bright pink, plastic-wrapped orb. "I need to film a product video for these fizzy bath bombs."

Amelia's wrath was in no way assuaged by this information. "Then I will return to my earlier question," she said coldly. "Why aren't you dressed?"

"Oh, Ames," said Kandyss. Her tone was mockingly condescending. "I don't get to have a hundred thousand people following me on social media by dressing like you do."

To my mind, this decision by Kandyss to go on the offensive seemed ill-conceived. Dudley's wide eyes showed that he thought so too.

"Get out," said Amelia. She pointed down the hall. Kandyss opened her mouth to speak again, but Amelia wasn't having it. "No," she said. "This whole conversation is over. You get out of this hallway before I kick you out of my house."

My heart sang.

Kandyss stormed back into the bathroom from whence she had come.

"What are you doing?" Amelia demanded. She advanced further down the hall to see for herself.

Dudley, overcome by a gentlemanly comprehension of the scene's impropriety, retreated into his office. He moved to a spot where he could still observe me as I watched the scene playing out before me. My reactions became his mirror. He indicated as much by signalling that I stay put. I was uncomfortable with the arrangement, but my feudal sensibilities obliged me to obey.

Kandyss reemerged from the bathroom. She was now wearing jeans under her bathrobe and was clutching a gym bag in her right hand. In her left she still held the bath bomb. "I'm getting my stuff," she hissed. "Is that okay with you? Is that okay that I'm getting *my* stuff out of *your* bathroom?"

Dudley, concealed as he was from the view of the combatants, made no effort to disguise his reactions. At this juncture, his was an expression of pure shock, and he seemed to be trying to draw his head back into his shoulders like a turtle retiring into its shell.

“Go,” said Amelia, struggling to remain calm. She pointed down the hall behind Kandyss.

“I’m going!” cried Kandyss. She began walking down the hall, but she did so backwards so that she could continue to fling vitriol during her retreat. “You don’t have to be such a bitch, Ames. It’s not my fault your husband came sneaking in like that.”

I saw something like a spasm run through Amelia. I wish I could have seen her face. Kandyss could see her face, and it seemed to frighten her. I should have liked to see what made her fingers tremble so violently that they dropped the bath bomb.

“What did you say?” Amelia asked. Her elegant hands were balled into small but deadly fists.

“That’s not true,” said Dudley, leaning out of his office. “There was no sneaking.”

“Why wouldn’t you knock on the door?” Kandyss cried.

“Because there wasn’t supposed to be anybody else up here but us three!” Dudley cried. The poor man was blushing fiercely as he made his defence. “Why wouldn’t you *lock* the door?”

“Because it’s a Saturday!” wailed Kandyss. “I didn’t think anybody would be using these offices!”

“Oh, well then!” cried Amelia with something between a laugh and a howl. “Then you might as well come up here—sneaking!—and film trash in our bathroom!"

"Oh, shut up, Ames!" snarled Kandyss. "I'm sure Dudley didn't see anything."

"That's true!" said Dudley hastily.

"Nothing much anyway." And here Kandyss chose to jeer at Amelia.

"Amy—" began Dudley. He was too late.

Amelia was off. I have commented previously on the abilities of my underbutler, Liam, as a runner. The two women before me gave such a display of athletic ability that my standards for sprinting prowess were raised considerably. As if reacting to a starter's pistol, both began to move at precisely the same moment and with a wonderful explosiveness of motion.

Kandyss was running for safety, which meant she had a long way to go. Amelia, however, was only running for the fizzy bath bomb where it lay on the hall floor. Her studies of the ancients no doubt helped her to recognise the value of ranged warfare. Not only did Amelia demonstrate her abilities as a runner in that upstairs hallway that day; the strength and accuracy of her arm was also proven. The woman could sling a stone at a hair and not miss.

The projectile struck Kandyss squarely between her shoulder blades, and a satisfying burst of pink dust marked the success of the shot. Kandyss squealed like a piglet and vanished from view, staggering slightly.

"Amy," said Dudley. "I didn't see anything. She started screaming before I even realised someone was in there, and I just—" Dudley put his hand over his eyes to demonstrate his reaction. "Right away. Back out the door. I—"

"We're done," said Amelia. "They're leaving today."

"Amy..."

I quickly withdrew into my office. In a daze, I felt my way back to my desk and sat down. My heart was pounding.

"No, I'm done. Did you see how she looked at me? I'm not having that woman walking around this house another day. And after we covered for her about the paintings!"

"I hear you. We're all upset. That was... that was crazy."

"Dudley. Call Lucifer right now. Tell him to start packing."

"I'm not going to do that, Amy."

"Oh? You're not?"

"Where would they go? We can't just put them in the street!"

"Oh, I think I could."

"Now Amy."

"No, Dudley. Don't 'now Amy' me. I'm serious. I've—" Amelia paused midsentence and stepped into my doorway. She said, "Sorry, Lancaster," and closed the door.

It was considerate of Mrs. Peterkin to spare me the particulars of what was rapidly becoming a proper fight. However, I should have preferred to be set loose into the garden before they got going rather than being shut in my office. No doubt she assumed that I would resume my work, but that was not the case. Instead, I sat there and listened to the excited voices of my beloved employers gradually rising higher and higher in desperation and volume. The longer I sat there, the more impossible it became for me to escape, as the scene I would be obliged to witness as I beat my retreat was becoming more and more emotional.

At long last the voices faded further still as Dudley (perhaps in consideration of my predicament) moved the conversation into his office and closed the door.

I made my escape both quickly and quietly.

* * *

Until that spring, I had never seen my employers fight. Now I was obliged to stand by and watch them warring like veterans. Children are often collateral damage when a couple has a falling-out. I do not wish to suggest that the relationship of children to their parents is similar to that of household domestics to their employers. Such a comparison would, clearly, be more than a little inappropriate and would probably excite the disapprobation of children and domestics alike. What I do mean to say is that for myself and the staff of Harper's Lane, having Dudley and Amelia on bad terms was profoundly distressing.

"They're sleeping in separate bedrooms," said Paige.

I cocked my head, surprised. "How do you know?"

"She spent almost two hours in here yesterday."

"Doing what?"

"What do you think?"

"Telling you about their sleeping arrangements, apparently."

Liam rose from the table. "I'm going to go check on the Tremblays," he said.

"Thank you, Mr. Hendrix." I turned back to Paige. "What did she say?"

"Eat your soup and I'll tell you."

I obeyed and she obliged.

"So first of all, the Peterkins asked Kandyss to apologise for trespassing and flashing Dudley and that whole fiasco."

"I don't believe there was any flashing," I said.

"Eat your soup."

"Right."

"So instead of apologising, Lucifer calls Dudley and says that they're the real injured party and I was like, "How?!" and Amelia said that apparently Lucifer claimed that because the Peterkins' plumbing had destroyed half his life's work, and because Amelia had 'assaulted' Kandy Kane with a bath bomb, they're lucky the Tremblays aren't suing them for everything they've got. So I said, 'Well, that's bull! Why don't you just point out that the damage to the paintings was all Wonder Woman's fault?' and Amelia said she wants to be the bigger woman and that it would seem petty to jump in and cover for Kandyss one day and then just throw her under the bus because she and Dudley are fighting."

I listened to these enormous run-on sentences in fascinated silence before interjecting. "But why are she and Mr. Peterkin still fighting?"

"I'm getting to that. Soup. So I said, 'Why are you and Dudley still fighting?' and she said that she wants Dudley to pull the trigger and relocate the Tremblays, but he won't because he says that he does actually feel guilty about how things have gone and he wants to see if this will blow over, and so she said, 'Well, until you see that those creeps are always going to be creeps and maybe you shouldn't have invited them to come and ruin our lives like an idiot, I'll be in the guest bedroom down the hall' and I said, 'good for you' because I think this is all on Dudley and he needs to grow a spine."

If it had been Liam speaking instead of Paige, I would have urged restraint. Instead, all I said was, "I see."

"So now it's a waiting game," continued Paige. Observing that I had just finished consuming one of the rolls with which she had served the soup, she passed me another. It is not relevant to the dialogue, but I must mention that those rolls were of her own creation. They were soft, white, and still hot, gleaming under a perfect glaze. I think I could have eaten them all, and I do not consider myself gluttonous.

"Thank you," I said, accepting the roll reverently.

"Sure. So who do you think will break first? Will the Tremblays see how awful they're being and apologise? Or will Dudley realise that he needs to stick by Amelia and kick them out?"

"Perhaps there's a third way," I mused.

"I don't see it."

"Are the Peterkins on speaking terms at all?"

"I don't think so. Speaking of which, Amelia asked me to tell you that she'll be taking her meals in her office for the foreseeable future."

"Seems a bit bleak," I said.

"Such is marriage," said Paige cynically.

"And what do you know of marriage, Miss Schopenhauer?" I asked.

"Mr. Lancaster. Are you calling me an old maid?"

"I'm sure I would never call you a maid."

Paige's foot caught me on the shin. "And what would *you* know of marriage, you old bachelor?"

"A thing or two," I said with affected self-assurance.

"More than me? You haven't been married any more than I have."

"The most expensive bottles are rarely opened."

"Oho!" Paige pitched a roll at me, which I was lucky enough to catch.

"Thank you," I said, holding my prize aloft. "I was hoping for another."

"You could have asked."

"I don't think I would have dared."

"Oh, is that why you never married?"

I opened my mouth, but no words came out. I laughed hoarsely.

When I took Mrs. Peterkin her dinner that evening, she appeared to be in high spirits. She beamed at me as I entered and removed her headphones. She swung her computer screen out of the way to make space on her desk for the tray I was carrying, muttering self-deprecating jokes about the state of her office. Once a spot was cleared, she looked up and smiled her eyes into a squint.

"Lancaster! Oh, thank goodness you're here."

I set her tray down and removed the cloche. "I have taken the liberty of bringing wine," I said, touching the small carafe on the tray. "You haven't had the Grenville Cab Franc Reserve in some time, and I thought it would be appropriate with tonight's dinner."

Amelia nodded her approval enthusiastically. "I can't wait! You spoil me, Lancaster."

"I hope so, Mrs. Peterkin." I decanted a glass of the wine, drew back from the desk, and stood at attention. I would wait a few minutes until she had eaten a bite or two before leaving. This would allow her an opportunity to let me know if she needed anything further.

"Paige never misses, does she?"

"She does not, ma'am."

"And how is Liam doing? Still working out all right?"

"Oh yes, Mrs. Peterkin. I am very pleased with his performance so far. He seems to possess the ability to find pride and joy in service. It is this quality that really makes the difference."

"Did you begin as an underbutler yourself, Lancaster?"

"I did not. When I was first offered a position in household management, I was a concierge."

"Did you have those little golden keys on your uniform?"

"I did enjoy the honour of that membership, yes."

"How do you get in? Is there a test of some kind? A hotel obstacle course you have to run? A triathlon of hospitality?"

"I had the privilege of being sponsored for the position by existing members. There was a process of examination, of course, and I was interviewed by a committee of existing Clefs d'Or members."

"How old were you?"

"I was twenty-two, ma'am."

"That's quite young. Were you nervous?"

"I'm sure that I was."

"How long had you been in hotels at that point?"

"Most of my life, ma'am. Three years as a concierge."

"What is the minimum for the keys?"

"Three years."

"So you applied as soon as you were able."

"Yes. The owner of the hotel was quite adamant."

"Do you ever think that..." Here Mrs. Peterkin trailed off. She was cradling her glass in both hands and appeared to have lost herself in watching the ripples that vexed the surface of the wine.

"Mrs. Peterkin?"

"I'm sure I'm being very talkative," she said quietly. "It's just that if I run out of questions to ask you, you'll leave."

I said nothing. It was true that I had to serve Mr. Peterkin's meal still.

"What is happening, Lancaster?"

I almost evaded the question. I opened my mouth to say, "I'm sure it's not my place to comment." The words hovered on my tongue... and then I closed my mouth. I straightened my tie. I turned one of my cufflinks. I looked up at Amelia. She was staring at me with her beautiful, trusting eyes. I remembered the first time I met her and how shy her smiling gaze had made me feel. Why don't more people make such simple, bold eye contact? I swallowed hard, opened my mouth, and started over.

"This is a hard season," I said gently. "They happen from time to time. They never last forever."

"Is that all it is? I'm so mad at Dudley, I could slap him."

"I am truly grieved to hear it."

"Has he always been like this? So incapable of jumping up and defending his own household? His own family?"

"Mrs. Peterkin. I have worked in seven countries, for nine employers, and have encountered thousands of powerful men in my career. Mr. Peterkin is a rare person. There is no one, present company excluded, who has a greater command of my loyalty."

Amelia folded her arms on the desk, rested her forehead against her wrist, and started sobbing pitifully.

I stepped forward quickly and reached for her shoulder. I hesitated. All this candour had forced me into uncharted waters. My fingertips came to rest on the desktop just short of her hand. I stood there, my heart aching with care, embarrassed by both my attempt and my inability to comfort this good woman.

Finally, the oppressive silence was broken by Amelia's soft voice. She didn't raise her head, and I had to lean closer to make out what she was saying.

"I know he's a good man, Lancaster, but is it possible that he's a weak man as well? He's always been so kind and generous, and I thought it was a strength."

"I'm sure your first instincts were correct," I said quickly.

She lifted her face from her arms but didn't look up at me. She was staring at my fingers where they still rested on the desk. "But it's not a strength to be nice if you are incapable of doing otherwise. The fact that he's letting the Tremblays walk all over us and humiliate his wife might seem like misplaced generosity, but now I wonder if he's actually just incapable of stopping them. Can Dudley really bring himself to say hard things that make people dislike him? I've always assumed that he could if he needed to, but now that I think about it, I'm usually the one who does that sort of thing. He's just..."

She looked at me as if I might finish her sentence.

I did not.

"You meet a man who never loses his temper or yells at people or gets into fights, and you think you've found a man who has learned restraint and self-control. What if you've simply met a man who *can't* do those things? It's not quite as impressive, is it?"

"Mrs. Peterkin."

"I'm sorry." Amelia sat up straight and took some tissues from a box on the desk.

"Please don't be sorry. Please stay strong. You have trusted Mr. Peterkin for all these years. I am sure he will show us all that your trust was well placed."

"I just want to go back to the way things were in March, Lancaster! It was such a terrible mistake inviting those people in here."

"You may be correct, ma'am."

Some people are very particular about the temperature at which sherry should be poured. While I agree that there is a general range of desirability and that it can vary somewhat from sherry to sherry, I refuse to credit the pedantry of those who insist that it must be served at precise degrees of temperature. I may be a Philistine, but I think that any differences detected between a sherry poured at fifty-eight degrees and one poured at fifty-five can be more readily attributed to the placebo effect than anything else.

"This sherry is too warm," said Hoffman testily.

I made no response and poured a taste into my own glass. As I tilted the crystal, I was pleased by the light amber colour of the sherry. It looked like an old chardonnay, but with edges the colour of maple syrup. I am content to be found unoriginal if it means I get to enjoy the comfort of the familiar. In this case, that meant always keeping a couple different Harveys VORS in the cellar.

"It's too warm," said Hoffman again.

"It's just right," I said firmly.

"Where do you keep it?"

"I have it in the little warmer whites fridge."

"You should put it in the freezer for a few minutes while we play."

"Would you like me to get you some ice?"

"Don't be a smartass." Hoffman was in a worse mood than usual.

"I beg your pardon."

Hoffman snorted and arranged his Rummikub tiles on their board. "What's going to happen with my daughter and her husband?"

"Are you asking for a prediction?"

"If that's all you've got." He waved at the table. "You go first."

I drew a tile. "I don't think the present tensions can persist for long."

"Completely useless," said Hoffman.

I sat back. "Are you feeling all right, sir?"

Hoffman started placing tiles on the table. "I'm just worried about Amelia."

"As am I, sir."

Hoffman looked past me. "What's that git doing?"

I glanced hurriedly over my shoulder. Liam, a collapsible chair in one hand and a box of jammy dodgers in the other, was approaching us across the lawn. We were set up in the back of the garden at the little iron table.

"Oh dear," I said.

"Is he trying to join us?" Hoffman asked.

"So it appears."

"Tell him to give us the cookies and piss off."

"Good evening, Mr. Hoffman!" cried Liam by way of greeting. He held his offering aloft. "I thought perhaps you gentlemen would like something to nibble on while you play." He snapped his chair into place but didn't sit. He knew better than to do so without permission. "I also thought that maybe you'd be interested in having a third for Rummikub."

Hoffman looked at me expectantly.

"Mr. Hendrix," I said. "You have been very thoughtful."

"Piss off," said Hoffman impatiently.

"I beg your pardon," said Liam. His colour rose.

"Mr. Hoffman and I have some sensitive household matters to discuss," I said.

"I apologise," said Liam. He collected the chair. "Enjoy the cookies," he said.

"Good man," said Hoffman.

Liam didn't acknowledge the parting compliment but walked away briskly, his ears bright.

When I returned to the cottage that night, Liam had already retired to his room. I could hear him playing a video game through his door. I considered knocking and apologising for the scene with Hoffman but decided against it. I would try to catch him in the morning instead.

(Tuesday, May 10)

Liam avoided me before and during breakfast service. Afterwards I saw him taking a walk under the fruit trees behind the East Wing. I still had some cleaning to do in the kitchen before Paige got in, but I decided I should take the opportunity that lay before me. It would be good to smooth things over with Liam before he vented to Paige.

"Mr. Lancaster," said Liam as I approached. His tone was neutral but respectful.

I got right to it. "Mr. Hendrix, I have been hoping to apologise for what occurred last night. Mr. Hoffman is not a civil man. He has a very constricted comfort zone and doesn't react well when he thinks it is being threatened."

Liam nodded. "I'm sorry too. I should have asked you in advance if it would be appropriate to join you instead of jumping in like that."

"Your actions were not unreasonable. You see me spending time with the gentleman on a regular basis. Of course, I would normally avoid that kind of relationship with a member of the household's family, but Mr. Hoffman has his own approach to such things. That said, you should know that he's no more civil with me than he was with you last night."

"Is it a difficult relationship for you?"

"It took getting used to. Broadly speaking, I wouldn't recommend it."

"I believe you." Liam seemed to be thinking deeply for a moment. "Things are a bit tense around here right now, aren't they?"

"Yes."

"Is it more appropriate to act like you're sympathetic to the... the atmosphere, or should we act like we haven't noticed anything's wrong?"

My conversation with Amelia the night before sprang to mind. I dismissed it. Even if it felt hypocritical, I wouldn't complicate my advice to Liam with nuanced circumstances. He wasn't ready for that yet.

"The latter," I said, "certainly. If a member of the household addresses their issues to you directly, then it becomes more complex, as neutrality in that situation can seem almost hostile. However, for most occasions, providing consistent service for our employers is how we care for them best. They have family and friends and therapists to help them solve their problems. They have us to make their household stable and smooth. The moment we get roped into their drama, we risk compromising our ability to perform our duty effectively. Instead of being comforted by the sight of us, they will wonder what we think about their personal affairs. They'll wonder if we think less of them. They'll become defensive with us—us!—their servants."

"Have you seen situations like that?"

"Many times."

"Boundaries."

"Boundaries indeed, Mr. Hendrix. They are essential to flourishing."

"Here comes Mrs. Tremblay."

Together we watched Kandyss approach. She was wearing a dress that seemed to be constructed of a hundred scraps of sheer fabric layered and draped over one another. It was a fluttering, misty cloud of mauve and green that made me nervous. I am sure that it was essentially modest by design, with the fabric cleverly layered to ensure the decency of the wearer, but this was not what it suggested to the viewer. To the viewer, it seemed to promise (or threaten) that at any moment its shifting folds might be arranged revealingly. Whenever Kandyss moved, I resisted the urge to avert my eyes.

"Liam!" sang Kandyss.

"Mrs. Tremblay," replied Liam. "May I be of service?"

"I need to talk to your boss," said Kandyss.

Liam nodded and trotted out of earshot.

"What a good boy," squeaked Kandyss admiringly. "Do you think he plays tennis, Lancaster?"

"As a matter of fact, I believe he does," I replied.

"Do you think he would teach me?"

"Was there something you wished to discuss with me, Mrs. Tremblay?"

"Don't be like *that,* Lancaster. Not today. I'm way too upset."

"I beg your pardon."

"What's going on in there?" She pointed at the West Wing. Her dress fluttered. I winced.

"What are you asking me, Mrs. Tremblay?"

"Does Amy still expect me to apologise?"

I decided to lock this door before it could be opened. I straightened my posture and lifted my chin. "It would be entirely inappropriate for me to acknowledge, let alone comment on such a matter."

"Don't be like that. You know those people. You know what they're saying. How am I supposed to know what to do if I don't know what they're thinking? If their marriage falls apart because I didn't know how to act, that's not my fault."

"Please excuse me, Mrs. Tremblay."

"No! Stay!"

I'm sure there was surprise on my face as I looked at her. I seriously considered just walking away, but my reflexive obedience held me fast. "Mrs. Tremblay?"

She stepped closer. I drew back my head. She was smiling. In a low voice that was almost a murmur, she said, "To think that I was jealous of that woman, Lancaster. So smart. So pretty. So rich. Look at Amelia Peterkin now. Losing her mind because her old man tried to take a peek at me. Maybe Mom was onto something after all. Hmm?"

I said nothing. I did not feel nothing.

Kandyss put her hand on my chest. "Lanny," she said softly. "Am I right? How's Amy doing? I hope I'm wrong! I hope she's not jealous."

I stepped back. Her hand fell to her side. She cocked her head and regarded me with an expectant smile. I clenched my teeth with every muscle in my jaw.

"Lancaster?"

"I will thank you to excuse me, Mrs. Tremblay."

And I left.

Lucian Tremblay asked me to meet with him after lunch. More precisely, he sent a note to me via Liam on which was scrawled, "Let's meet at 2:00. Stuff to talk about. See you then."

"What do you think he wants?" Paige asked.

"I'm sure I don't know."

"Are you nervous?"

"Why should I be?"

Paige looked up at me thoughtfully. "I don't know," she said. "I just get the sense that there's an ominous shift happening. Like the Tremblays have the upper hand. They can do whatever they want. It's like they run this house now. Or at least think they do."

I tried not to scold. "Miss Schopenhauer," I said, "let's avoid becoming dramatic."

"You think I'm wrong."

"I do."

Paige was not, as it turned out, wrong.

"Please," said Lucian with a magnanimous smile, "take a seat."

We were in the East Wing's library. Kandyss was nowhere to be seen, but I could hear her moving about in the rooms above my head.

"Thank you, sir." I sat in a chair that was, coincidentally, the one I used to sit in when this library was the evening haunt of Hoffman and myself. Lucian was sitting in Hoffman's usual armchair.

"Lancaster. Buddy." Lucian smiled at me with an affected fondness in his dark eyes.

The eyes of that man studied mine with an insolent boldness. The image of Amelia sobbing in her office had been haunting me all day. Both she and Lucian were pleased to look me right in the eyes. Both filled me with emotion. In Amelia's office I had found myself putting aside professionalism for the sake of that emotion. Here, with this serpent grinning into my soul, I found myself shrugging off my principles once more.

"What's your first name, Lancaster?"

"I am afraid that I have forgotten it, sir."

Lucian maintained his smile, but the furious contempt with which he usually regarded me seemed to hover behind his thin-lipped grin. We examined one another for a long moment, our eyes silently communicating in the war songs of old.

"The reason I called you over here," said Lucian, turning the conversation to matters of business, "is to discuss some changes to our breakfast arrangements."

"Very good, sir." I procured my notebook and opened it to a clean page. My Parker 51 hovered, poised to faithfully record Lucian's every request.

"From now on," the artist began, "we will have a hot breakfast served at ten. If we want it earlier, we'll call Liam earlier. If we want it later, we'll tell Liam to bring it later."

"Mr. Tremblay," I began carefully, "I believe we have discussed the dynamics that constrain the kitchen here."

"Did you understand what I said?" Lucian asked.

"I believe that I understand the nature of your request, yes."

"I ask because you didn't write it down."

"Well, sir—"

"And it wasn't a request. Write it in your little black book, Lancaster. Ten o'clock. Write ten o'clock."

I wrote a large "10" on the page and closed my notebook. "Thank you, Mr. Tremblay. I will discuss the matter with Mr. Peterkin."

Lucian seemed to brighten. "Why? Why would you discuss it with Mr. Peterkin?"

"There is a contract that lays certain restrictions on your use of Mr. Peterkin's staff. I would want to see that he permits the domestic alteration you have requested."

"I didn't request anything. Did I say, 'I have a *request'*? Did I say, 'here's my *request*, Lancaster?'"

"You did not, sir."

"Did you hear me use the word *request* at all today?"

"I naturally comprehend the spirit in which you are addressing me, Mr. Tremblay. However, the substance of your directions must take the form of a request until authorised by the Peterkins."

Lucian leaned forward. "Kandyss told me you weren't very helpful when she asked how things stood with the Peterkins. I told her you were just being snotty, but maybe I was wrong. Maybe you really don't get it."

"I'm sure I don't know what you mean," I said.

I was taken aback by the man's confidence. A certain dread settled into my gut as I remembered Paige's words from our conversation that morning. I now saw that her assessment had been closer to the truth than I had imagined. Clearly, first with Kandyss and now with Lucian, the Tremblays were trying to evaluate me as a threat to their coup.

Lucian sat back, and his smile returned. "Let me lay it out for you, sweetheart. Kandyss and I live here now. We are your employers as much as the Peterkins. Now, that might sound crazy. You're thinking, 'What's that, Mr. Tremblay? Aren't you just a guest? A nobody artist? A bum who leeches off my billionaire boss?' Well, Lancaster, think again. That contract you mentioned. What do you think Dudley is going to do if I just tear it up? Do you think he'll evict me?"

Lucian baited me with a long pause. I opened my mouth to speak, and he cut me off sharply.

"He wouldn't. He wouldn't *dare,* honey. I'd sue him for millions just like that." Lucian snapped his fingers. "We were dragged out here to satisfy that idiot's vanity. Then we were treated like second-class citizens, like pets being kept for his amusement. Even his fabulous little butler was bossing us around and sneering at us from Day One. No!" Lucian held up his hand and shook his head wearily. "Don't apologise. I know it's not your fault. You're an extension of Dudley's little vanity empire, just like me.

"But then what happens? His cheap plumbing destroys my life's work. Hundreds of thousands of dollars in art damaged or destroyed. The entire record of my journey as a torchbearer in this wild new century pissed on by his tacky mansion. There's no way to put a price tag on that, but let's just say that, by all rights, I should own this house.

"So what happens next? My wife decides to try out a bathroom on the other side of the house. Amelia is so outraged by Kandy *daring* to stray out of her pen that she literally assaults her. Can you imagine how this whole story would look in court? Do you think Amelia would want to explain that she attacked Kandy because she's made insecure by having a famous model in the house? Do you think that Dudley would want to be put under oath and explain that he evicted us after he got caught playing Peeping Tom?"

Lucian sat back and ran his tongue across his lips with reptilian swiftness. His attitude was one of pure delight. His eyes raked back and forth across my person as he sought any indication of how I might be taking his little speech.

I considered walking out without saying anything. I had considered doing so several times during his outrageous account of the past couple months. I also considered more unhinged, violent solutions. Ultimately, I simply tucked my notebook and pen back into my inner pocket without saying a word.

"Well?" said Lucian.

"I will communicate your request to Mr. Peterkin," I said. I rose from my seat.

"Really?" Lucian also rose. "Really, Lancaster? Come on, man! Don't you ever get tired of being such a perfect little toady? It disgusts me that people like you still exist, honestly. You realise that you're little better than livestock to those people? Your job is a joke. You do regular crap that normal people do so that your *masters* can feel like gods. It's disgusting. Your existence couldn't possibly be more purposeless. It's the twenty-first century, and you're crawling around living some pervy little slave fantasy."

It was irritating to hear the man who had been delighting in talking down to me at the outset of our interview now expressing concern about my role as a domestic. I tugged at my coat and adjusted my stance. I straightened my glasses on my nose.

"Well?" said Lucian again.

"Mr. Tremblay," I said, "I think you may underestimate your own intelligence."

Lucian seemed open to this idea. He tilted his head, considering. "How so?"

"You will recall, sir, that I was present when it was discovered your paintings had been regrettably damaged by water."

"Okay?"

"And you will recall, sir, that your first instinct was to go and inspect the bathroom above your studio."

"That's right."

"Perhaps, sir, you should have trusted your own intuition more."

"Oh?"

"Perhaps there would be value in asking Kandyss why she needed to use the bathroom in the Peterkins' quarters."

Lucian's expression was becoming darker with every word that I spoke. "Oh really?"

"I only said perhaps."

"I see." Lucian studied my face closely. "Why are you telling me this? Are you defying your masters? Is this Lancaster's first step toward freedom?"

"As to that, Mr. Tremblay." I looked into his eyes and tried to imagine a point twenty inches past his head and focus on that instead. "I reserve the right to find satisfaction in my work, whether or not you understand it. We all have roles to fill on life's stage. I will thank you not to begrudge me the simple dignity of pursuing excellence in the performance of my duties."

Lucian started talking, but trailed off as I took my leave.

When I arrived at Dudley Peterkin's office door, he was sitting with his head in his hands. Though some in the household blamed the present distress on Dudley's character, I still pitied the man. I had not respected my employer for years only to harbour contempt for him now. I knocked on the door frame.

Dudley looked up and waved me in. "Lancaster. Please. Feel free to shut the door behind you."

I did so. "Mr. Peterkin," I said. "I have a matter to discuss with you."

"Anything, Lancaster!"

I shared Lucian Tremblay's request regarding future breakfasts.

"You told him it's not a restaurant?"

"Not in so many words, sir, but I did make him aware that the house practices regular mealtimes."

"And?"

"He was not open to discussing the matter. He was very careful to let me know that it wasn't a request."

"Oh, he was, was he!" Dudley seemed quite provoked by the idea. "Leave this with me, Lancaster. In the meantime, carry on as you were before."

"Thank you, sir." I turned to go.

"Lancaster?"

I paused and regarded my employer. A great many people had bravely chosen to be vulnerable with me in recent hours, and something about the set of Dudley's jaw suggested that I was about to enjoy another round. He looked as though he were on the verge of saying the words, "man to man."

"Sir?"

"I don't want to make you uncomfortable, Lancaster."

"Thank you, sir."

"You have served Amelia and me so well over the past few years. You know us pretty well at this point."

"It has been a privilege."

"Lancaster, I need someone who understands things the way you do to give me advice. Can we... can we just suspend some of the aloofness for a few minutes?"

"Sir?"

"I want to speak freely with you. Man to man."

There it was.

I was starting to get used to this. I repressed the urge to polish my glasses. "As you wish, sir."

"Really?"

"Desperate times, sir."

"Wow, Lancaster. Thanks." Dudley heaved a sigh. "Here's the deal. I'm struggling to know what to do. I don't want to treat the Tremblays badly, but Amy's absolutely set on me ending our relationship with them. You probably know that much already."

"Yes."

"She's not kidding around, Lancaster. We're on the rocks."

"I'm sorry to hear it."

"And the thing is, I know she's right. This whole patronage nonsense was such a terrible idea! What was I thinking? How could I be so *silly?* It was all vanity, Lancaster! Inviting strangers—nothing more than strangers!—into our house was completely insane! And now we're stuck. We're having to tiptoe around the Tremblays. I have a kind of responsibility to them, but I also need to protect my marriage!"

"A difficult scenario, sir."

"And now even Amy's snapped. She's such a good sport, Lancaster. You know that. It takes a lot to make that woman put her foot down. I need to fix this mess, but how?"

"I'm sure that Mrs. Peterkin has a recommendation or two," I hazarded.

"You can say that again. She thinks I should write them an eviction notice. Buy a month or two in a hotel room somewhere back in New York, put them on a plane, and let them find a new place from there."

"I see."

"Should I do it?"

"Are you barred from doing so by the terms of the contract between you and Mr. Tremblay?"

"Not technically. We're well within the probationary trial period. I can still terminate without cause, and they have three weeks to get out. I think they'd go for it. Especially if I gave them an allowance during that period."

"I see."

"And I *would* pull the trigger," said Dudley hurriedly, "but I just keep considering it from their perspective. I proposed this whole arrangement. They didn't ask to be relocated. I suggested it. Things went poorly, and they're being sent back to Square One, except now they have to find a new home, and all the paintings he came here with are water damaged."

"It is worth remembering that you are not to blame for the damage to his paintings."

"Right. He doesn't know that."

"Well." I looked up at the ceiling. "He might still find out."

"He might."

"Mr. Peterkin," I said. "You have asked me to speak to you as man to man."

Dudley brightened. "Yes!"

"I applaud your concern for the Tremblays."

"I'm just trying to do the right thing by them."

"That's commendable. Now forget about them entirely. If your relationship with that couple falls apart, it has much more to do with their failings than yours. You are not responsible for its collapse. You are, however, entirely responsible for the damage being done to your marriage."

"Oof," said Dudley.

"Oof indeed, sir. If I may be so bold, I believe that you have allowed yourself to become derailed."

"Derailed."

"Derailed, sir. You think that Mr. Tremblay offers you something worth having. You think he makes you more sophisticated. You think he is unlocking an exciting new chapter in your life."

"I am only trying to do the right thing," said Dudley. He looked angry.

"No, you are not."

"Lancaster," said Dudley in a warning tone.

"Man to man," I said. "That is how you asked me to address you."

"Right."

"And man to man, I think you are trying to have your cake and eat it too. You are right when you say that your vanity has led you astray. You thought Mr. Tremblay might help you achieve some new variety of fame. Now, even when that vision has proven silly, you're so afraid of having someone dislike you that you can't bring yourself to put your foot down. You're not struggling to know what to do. You already know your duty, but instead you're trying to find a way to keep the peace with the Tremblays without having to face any consequences in your relationship with Mrs. Peterkin. You can't grasp at fire and hope not to get burned, but that's exactly what you're doing."

"It's not that simple."

"I'm sorry, sir, but I think it might be."

"I'm not just being selfish, though. I have thought about kicking them out, Lancaster. I've considered everything you're saying, but what if things have gone too far? Sure, I've screwed up, but if I try to back out now, the Tremblays might continue to ruin our lives. They might try suing. They might dox us. I want to back out of my mistake, but how do I do it without making an even bigger mess?"

"I will think on it, sir, but you must be the one to arrive at the final solution. Your wife has been watching you shirk your duty for far too long."

"Hey now."

"I beg your pardon, sir."

"No. You're right." He put his head back in his hands, just as he had been when I entered.

"I know you to be a kind and diplomatic man," I said, assuming a gentler tone. "But sometimes even kind men and diplomats must accept risks for the sake of those they love."

Dudley was about to reply when a knock sounded on the door. We looked at one another sharply. I have no doubt that we both wondered if it might be Mrs. Peterkin and if she had perhaps heard any part of our discussion.

"Come in!" called Dudley.

It was not the lady of the house after all.

"Sorry to interrupt," said Paige. "I was just looking for Mr. Lancaster."

"You've found him!" said Dudley with a smile.

She stepped closer to me, gesturing with her phone. "I sent you the dinner menu. You didn't respond."

I fumbled in my coat for my phone. "I beg your pardon, Miss Schopenhauer. I didn't feel it vibrate."

"Do you need to go?" Dudley asked.

"Not at all." I glanced quickly at the menu. "I will probably pour the Tracey Vineyards Sauvignon Blanc. I should just double-check that there's a bottle in the fridge."

"I can check for you," said Paige. "I don't want to interrupt your meeting."

"Would you? That would be so kind. It's the bottle with the purple label and the little—"

"I know the one." Paige pinched my arm. "You owe me." She nodded to Dudley as she backed out of the office. "Sorry again for interrupting, sir."

Once more, we were alone. Dudley was the first to speak.

"Kind men, diplomats, *and* butlers, Lancaster?"

"Sir?"

My employer rose. He was still flushed from the excitement of our conversation, but Paige's interruption had given him a moment to calm down. "It couldn't have been easy, but you've done me a real favour speaking your mind like that, Lancaster."

"I hope I didn't overdo it, sir."

"No."

"What will you do?"

"I don't know. I guess I'll sleep on it."

"Wise," I said. "When the time to speak hard truths comes upon us, it is generally best to sleep at least once before beginning. Or so my mother used to tell me."

"Was your mother wise?"

"I have always thought so."

"Let's go with that then. Thanks again, Lancaster."

(Wednesday, May 11)

Shortly after two in the morning, I was awakened by the sound of the property's security system. There was a speaker for the alarm in the warden's cottage, and it was far louder than necessary. As I staggered into the hall, buttoning my trousers and blinking furiously, I nearly collided with Liam. The underbutler was wearing only his boxers.

"What's going on?" Liam shouted above the sound of the alarm's wail.

"Someone's triggered the alarm!" I replied. "Put some clothes on!"

I half-staggered, half-jogged toward the house, buttoning my shirt as I went. All the house's exterior lights were on, and I was nearly blinded by them as I approached the back door. It was because of this that I didn't see the shadowy figure that came leaping down the gazebo steps just as I was mounting them.

I found myself lying on the dew-soaked grass, staring at the stars. The wind had been knocked out of me, as they say, and I very briefly struggled to draw a breath. After a panicked, prolonged moment, fresh air rushed into my lungs, and I was able to express myself. As I lay there, groaning like a floorboard and just as flat, my view of the stars was obstructed by the figure of Liam Hendrix bending over me.

"Mr. Lancaster! Did you fall?"

"Help me up," I croaked.

Liam propped me against the low stone wall beside the steps. I was pleased to see that he was dressed less like a Calvin Klein model than he had been minutes before.

"Are you okay?"

I nodded.

"Did you fall?"

I shook my head.

"What happened?"

I pointed at the steps. "I was knocked down. Some bastard came ripping down the stairs and knocked me over."

"Who?"

"Didn't see."

"Where did he go?"

"How should I know?" I snapped. "I was on my back!"

"Right." Liam nodded vigorously. It was clear that he was still trying to wake up.

"Come on," I said gruffly. "Let's go see what's going on inside."

As we entered the house, we were greeted by shouts from Dudley Peterkin, who was busy disengaging the alarm. "Hey! Did you see anybody going out when you were coming in?"

"Did I ever."

The alarm died.

"I beg your pardon?" Dudley asked, his voice still raised.

"Mr. Lancaster was knocked down on his way in," explained Liam.

"Are you hurt?"

I shook my head.

Amelia leaned over the banister above our heads. "Is everyone okay?"

"I hope so!" replied Dudley. "There was an intruder. He knocked down Lancaster!"

"Ha!" snorted Hoffman, who was slowly descending the staircase.

Amelia ran downstairs, and perhaps predictably, gave me a hug. My back protested under the pressure of the embrace, and I groaned.

"You're hurt!" cried Amelia.

"Hardly," I assured her.

"And you're all wet," Hoffman observed.

"Just the dew."

"Get in that chair over there right now," said Amelia

"Oh no," said I.

"Oh yes!" said Dudley. "Amy's absolutely right. Liam, get Lancaster something to drink."

"Oh *really,"* I protested feebly.

Overpowered, I allowed Dudley and Amelia to lead me into the sitting room and arrange my various parts in a voluminous armchair. Though they were now talking and cooperating, that persistent chill still hovered between them. Even as they worked together to make me feel as embarrassed as humanly possible, they were hampered by an awkward formality.

Dudley's phone rang.

"It's Lucifer. Hello? Lucy?"

Liam entered the room holding a glass of water. He offered it to me. I glared at him. Hoffman took the glass from Liam and drew a long, sucking gulp of water. Liam shrugged.

"There was an intruder," Dudley was saying. "He's gone. Okay. Yeah. Okay. Well, I've told the security company that there was an intrusion, and the police are on their way. Okay. Good thinking. Bye."

Dudley hung up.

"Are they okay?" Amelia asked.

"They've barricaded themselves in their room. Apparently, Lucifer is the one who triggered the alarm. He said he caught somebody snooping around in their dining room."

"That's crazy!" said Amelia. She shivered suddenly. "I don't like that at all."

Dudley gazed at his wife wistfully. He wanted to give her a hug. It must have felt unnatural not to, yet presumptuous to attempt it. Instead, he turned his attention back on me.

The police confirmed that there was nobody else lurking in the house. Whoever had knocked me down on the back steps seemed to have been the only intruder. I was interviewed at length about my encounter with the shadowy figure, but it was finally agreed that I was useless. I had really seen nothing at all worth discussing.

The Tremblays were able to contribute more to the investigation. They had piled all their bedroom furniture against the door, but were eventually extracted from their room and added to the fray.

It was a frosty conference. The Peterkins weren't the only couple acting distant with one another. The Tremblays stood about as far apart as they could without one of them leaving the room. I wondered if Lucian had talked with Kandyss about the bathroom situation.

When Lucian said that he was the first to see the intruder, he received the full attention of the police officer in charge.

"Tell me exactly what happened," the officer said, tapping a notepad with his pen.

"I heard the back door," explained Lucian. "I went downstairs and saw somebody sneaking around. I hit the alarm button on the panel and ran back upstairs."

"Would you be able to describe this person?"

"About my height," said Lucian.

The officer sized him up. “Five eight?”

Lucian adjusted his posture. “Five ten and a half.”

The officer nodded. “Very exact. Anything else?”

“It was dark. I couldn’t see his face.”

“Okay.”

“He wasn’t obese.”

“Okay.”

“Are you going to write that down?”

“Would you describe him as being of athletic build? Average? Skinny?”

“Not obese.”

The officer chewed on the inside of his cheek. “Naw. I’m not going to write that down. Anything else?”

“Male.”

“Male.”

“Probably.”

“How probably?”

Lucian shrugged.

“Okay. Thank you, Mr. Trembly.”

“Tremblay.”

“Did I spell that wrong?” The officer held up his pad.

“No, you just pronounced it wrong. The ‘a’ isn’t silent.”

“Okay. Thank you.”

“I notice that you didn’t write down any of my description of the perpetrator.”

“Person, five eight, not obese, possibly male.” The officer tapped his temple. “Like a steel trap.” He turned to Kandyss. “Did you see anything, ma’am?”

Kandyss, wearing something ghastly and pistachio-coloured, shook her head and assumed a pouty face for reasons best known to herself.

"Is that a no?"

"I stayed in my room," said Kandyss. "When Lucy told me there was someone in the house, we just got busy putting stuff against the door and stayed safe." She looked at Amelia defensively. "I didn't share my location or anything. It wasn't my fault this time."

The officer perked up. "This time?"

Hoffman looked at me. I looked away.

"Was there a previous incident of the same nature?" the police officer asked.

"Sort of," said Dudley. "We had someone on the grounds taking pictures of the house a couple months ago. Lancaster can tell you more about that."

The police officer turned to me expectantly. In fact, every last person in the room seemed to be affording me their attention.

"He was a young man," I said. "I had completely forgotten about him. He found our location on one of Mrs. Tremblay's social media posts—"

"Oh! I said *sorry!*"

"Please," said the officer, holding up his hand to silence the incensed Kandyss.

"I was with Mr. Hoffman and Mr. Hendrix at the time." Here the officer stopped me and pointed at Hoffman and Liam respectively to confirm the identities of the story's cast members. I nodded, and he waved me on. "Mr. Hendrix was able to catch the boy in question and—"

"Boy? You said young man before. How old was this person?"

"Oh!" I looked at Hoffman and he looked away. "Fifteen? Sixteen?"

"Really?" Liam sounded surprised.

"You disagree?" the officer asked encouragingly. "Would you like to suggest a different age?"

"Early twenties."

"Early twenties. Does that seem possible, Mr. Lancaster?"

"Older," said Hoffman.

The officer pointed at the old man like an auctioneer accepting a new bid. "How old?"

"Late thirties," said Hoffman.

Dudley looked baffled.

"Late *thirties!"* cried the officer. "Fifteen? Early twenties? Late thirties? Quite the range."

"Are you sure, Dad?" Amelia asked gently.

"Positive," said Hoffman.

"Okay," said the officer. "What about his appearance? Skin colour? Hair colour? Tattoos? Piercings?"

"Caucasian," said Liam.

"Southeast Asian," said Hoffman.

"He was white," I said, nodding to Liam. "With brown hair."

"I thought it was bleached white with dark roots," said Liam.

"Bald as an egg," said Hoffman enthusiastically. "His whole scalp tattooed with a likeness of the Malayan sun bear."

"I can't remember any tatts," said Liam, who was looking more and more bewildered.

"One on the inside of his right forearm," I said. "An eagle with spread wings. He was also wearing a Harley Davidson ring."

"I can't remember if he had jewellery," said Liam faintly.

"Five silver chains," said Hoffman. "Maybe six."

A silence fell. The officer was writing furiously. He looked up at last, his eyes narrow. "Conflicting accounts," was all he said.

"But was he obese?" asked Lucian.

We all agreed that the individual in question was not, in fact, obese.

"Sounds like the guy I saw," said Lucian.

"Only if the guy you saw happened to be three entirely different people," said the officer dryly.

"You know," Liam gestured toward Hoffman, "we could just look at your phone, Mr. Hoffman. You took a picture of him."

Hoffman looked at me. I looked away.

The officer turned to Dudley. "Excuse me," he asked in a fatigued voice, "but could you possibly get me a glass of water?"

"You took a picture of him, Dad?" Amelia was looking a little embarrassed.

"Yes," said Hoffman. "On my phone."

"That's great," said the officer.

"But that was months ago," said Hoffman.

"So?"

"I don't have that phone anymore."

"It might be on the, uh... on a cloud service of some kind. Right? Do you have a way to access the photos that you had on that phone?"

"Dad," said Amelia, "when did you get rid of your phone?"

"I didn't."

During this exchange, I had a bizarre experience. I made eye contact with Kandyss, and for the briefest moment, we were on the same page. We were both just struggling to keep up with a conversation that was rapidly coming to read like an Abbott and Costello script. She saw the confusion in my expression and nodded, as much as to say, “I know, right?”

“Mr. Hoffman,” said the officer, taking the glass of water Dudley offered him, “do you still have the phone on which you took a picture of the intruder?”

“No.”

“Why not?”

“It was stolen.”

This revelation rocked the room. Amelia and Dudley stared at each other with expressions of concern. Lucian started raising his voice for no apparent reason. Liam had assumed a stiff, domestic posture and seemed to be heeding my advice about staying detached from the affairs of the household. The officer began doing breathing exercises between sips of water. I glanced at Kandyss again to see if there was more commiseration to be had there, but I found that she had begun to cry. I looked at Hoffman. He looked away.

In the end, Dudley and Amelia withdrew to another room with the officer and, I believe, informed him that Mr. Hoffman was senile. Whatever they told him, things were quite streamlined after that. Phone or no phone, the officer no longer seemed interested in discussing the intruder incident from March.

The only remaining question was whether the intruder had stolen anything.

"I have no idea," said Dudley, looking around.

"The painting!" cried Lucian. He sprinted from the room.

"Is there a painting of great value in the house?" the officer asked.

"Yes," said Kandyss.

"No," said Hoffman.

The officer gave Hoffman a dirty look and waited for Dudley or Amelia to respond.

"Lucifer has been working on a painting," said Amelia, "but I don't think anyone would steal it."

"Not valuable?"

"I don't think anyone would know it exists," said Dudley, avoiding the question.

"Fine," said the officer. "Why don't we do a quick look around for missing electronics, money, or art."

A very cursory search was conducted. It is an awkward business, to look in a room for the absence of anything. It didn't take long before everyone agreed that the house looked very much the way it had the evening before.

"I'm going to let you all go back to bed," said the officer. "Get some good sleep. Search the house again in the morning. Here's my card. If you find that something's been stolen, call me." He collected his coat and headed for the front door. He looked back at the knot of discombobulated, alarmed people watching his departure and smiled. "Remember," he said. "That guy who knocked over your butler was by himself and running full tilt. Don't try reporting any stolen grand pianos or anything like that."

Exit the Law.

By that time, it was six o'clock in the morning. The Tremblays and Hoffman returned to their respective beds, but the Peterkins, Liam, and I decided that we might as well get started on our day.

By ten, Dudley, Amelia, and I were all in our offices with the doors open. I have mentioned before that this was our preferred way of working.

"Lancaster," Dudley called, "do you mind coming here for a minute?"

I joined my employer. "Sir."

He waved at the door. I shut it.

"I was thinking more about the conversation we had yesterday."

"I see."

"The thing is—"

A knock sounded at the door.

"Come in!" Dudley called.

The door swung upon.

Dudley scrambled to his feet. "Amy! Lancaster, could you give us—"

"No," said Amelia. "Lancaster needs to know this too. I just want to tell you that I've arranged to stay with my brother for a bit."

"When?"

"My flight leaves tomorrow morning."

"For how long?"

"I don't know."

Dudley choked. "Amy."

Amelia looked at her husband with dry eyes. "Dudley?"

"Just hang on."

"No."

"I know what's going on. I just—"

Amelia cut him off. She spoke in a steady, practiced way, as if she had said these words to herself a hundred times. "This isn't my home anymore. I can't live like this. This isn't what we agreed to build together. I can't always be the bigger person. I can't always be the one who stays calm and waits for everyone else to start behaving themselves."

Dudley started circling his desk to approach his wife, but she held up a hand. He stood still, frozen in horror, his face white. If his hands weren't fidgeting awkwardly, he might have resembled a statue of marble.

Amelia closed the door.

I quickly collected Dudley's chair and brought it to him. I took his arm. "Why don't you take a seat, sir."

He pushed me away forcefully and remained standing, one hand on his desk, the other clutching his stomach. Colour was returning to his face.

"Get out, Lancaster."

As I stepped into the hall, I was nearly bowled over by a pair of roving Tremblays.

"Piss off, Lancaster," said Lucian with his customary sneer. He and Kandyss pushed into Dudley's office without knocking.

I slowly made for my office.

"Lucifer! Kandyss!" Dudley's tone almost sounded hospitable, but I remembered his expression and felt a chill. "Were you able to get a little sleep?"

"We now know what was stolen," Lucian announced theatrically. He paused for effect.

I reached my office and looked across the hall at Amelia. She had put her headphones on and was missing this new development. I thought perhaps she shouldn't. I waved to get her attention, but she didn't notice.

"Oh? What was it?" Dudley asked.

I stepped into Amelia's office and gave her a panicked look. Amelia leapt up in surprise and pulled off her headphones. I held my finger to my lips and signalled that I was listening by cupping a hand behind my ear. She joined me in doing so.

"I'm only surprised that I didn't think to check if it was there last night," said Lucian, apparently building suspense.

"My tablet," announced Kandyss. "It's gone!"

Amelia somehow gasped without making a sound.

"Your tablet?" Dudley's voice was confused.

"Yes," said Lucian.

"Like… an iPad?"

Lucian laughed, angrily. "The artifact," he said. "The gift I bought for Kandyss."

"It's gone?"

"Vanished," Lucian confirmed.

"Let's give the police a call right away," said Dudley. "I have the officer's card right here."

"You could," Lucian drawled, "or maybe there's another option."

Amelia frowned. I frowned. I assume that Dudley frowned, but I couldn't see him.

"That's right," said Kandyss. "You could just get Amelia to give it back."

I clutched the doorframe. Amelia's jaw dropped, and she seemed to be screaming silently.

She looked like a whale shark suction feeding, if whale sharks were very pretty.

"I beg your pardon?" Dudley asked. His voice was quiet, but I could tell he was speaking from the chest.

"Tell her to give it back," whined Kandyss.

"Sorry," said Dudley. "Just to be clear, you're accusing Amy of stealing that stone?"

"It was her that I saw," said Lucian. "Five ten, slim, sneaking around our dining room in the middle of the night. I was asking myself, 'How did the thief get in when there was no sign of forced entry?' Well. Now we know."

"I assure you," said Dudley. "Amelia would never steal that thing. She doesn't even think it's authentic."

Lucian snorted. "Do you think she cares?"

"I do," said Dudley. "She's not a kleptomaniac. I think that if she suddenly turned to a life of crime, she would need some kind of motive."

Amelia shook her head at me. She rose and moved around her desk so she could hear better. She stood just inside the office, holding the door frame and listening.

"Oh," said Kandyss with something like a giggle. "She has a motive all right."

"And what might that be?" Dudley's voice was still calm. I wondered if he was standing or not.

"Think about it, buddy," said Lucian. "This has all been about our women and their little cage match. Kandyss feels insecure because Amy's smart. I get her a bougie gift and disrupt the balance between them. Now Kandy's the hot model *and* she's got a classy gewgaw. Suddenly Kandyss is the woman of the house. Why else would Amy cover for her when Kandy's bath ruined my paintings?"

Amelia and I gaped at one another, incredulous. Lucian continued.

"Then. Boom. Amy's worst nightmare. She catches you sneaking around after Kandy. She does what comes naturally to her. She tries to restore her idea of a proper order. If Kan is going to take something from her, she's going to take something back. It's her turn to sneak."

Lucian stopped talking. My eyes were narrow, and I was shaking my head. In my mind's eye, I could readily imagine just how smug the artist must be looking. Amelia looked ready to cry with pure rage.

"Is that so?" said Dudley evenly.

"You know I'm right, Dud. Don't pretend that Amy's above being—"

"First of all," said Dudley, "get your hands off my desk."

Amelia raised her eyebrows. So did I. There was something in Dudley's voice that excited us both.

"Here's the thing," said Lucian.

"No," Dudley said. "You're done explaining things to me, Lucifer Tremblay. You think this is a story about Amy and Kandyss squabbling? I have news for you. This is a story about a miserable, half-rate artist and his ability to twist narratives to suit him. It's a story about this lunatic being given an immense opportunity and squandering it."

"I—" said Lucian.

"Shut up!" bellowed Dudley. "You will not speak, Lucifer, unless I give you permission. You dare—you *dare*—to come swaggering into my office and accuse Amelia of stealing your pathetic antique? You have the nerve to talk about my wife as if she's some gorilla competing for a mate? She welcomed you into our home so you can pursue your art, and you think you're somehow in a position to sneer at her? To describe her the way you just did? You idiot. A thousand empires will rise and fall before Amelia Peterkin will have any reason—*any*—to be jealous of Kandyss Tremblay.

"Now. I'm glad you came barging in here like this, because I have some news for you. We're through, Lucifer. I'm evicting you. Pack your bags. I'll buy you a month at a hotel and give you one more month of your usual allowance. After that, you won't see a dime from me. You blew it, you twisted, nasty little man. You blew it."

"Oh," said Kandyss (with sass), "I don't think you want to do that."

"Why not?" Dudley asked sharply. The question was rhetorical. "Because of the damage *you* did to your husband's paintings? Clearly, we're all on the same page about that incident. We defended you for the same reason we've done everything for you: out of kindness. As with every other kindness we've offered you, you chose to repay it with pettiness and ingratitude.

"Or maybe you think I wouldn't want to evict you because Amy threw soap at you when you decided to come over to our offices, strip in our bathroom, and taunt Amy. You've certainly not sustained any physical injury, but if you think that Amy's behaviour was somehow more inappropriate than your own, then just take us to court.

"And while we're on the subject of that incident, I don't want to hear you talking about it the way you did a minute ago, Lucifer. There was no sneaking. I wasn't trying to see your wife. I needed to urinate. I was using my bathroom. I had no idea that Kandyss would be in there *with the door unlocked.* I'm a gentleman, Lucifer. I have never and will never betray Amy. You ever talk about my wife and I like that again, and I'll do more than throw soap at you—I'll use it to wash out your mouth."

There was a good deal of stammering from the Tremblays. Lucifer started raising his voice, but his words were incoherent: "Oh yeah! Yeah! Sure! Well! Think about that though! Hear yourself!"

The sound of something fragile shattering against the wall exploded from Dudley's office.

Silence fell. Amelia looked very excited.

"Your mug!" whispered Kandyss shakily.

When Dudley spoke again, his voice was so quiet that Amelia and I were both obliged to step into the hall outside his office door to make out what he was saying. "Maybe," he said, "you think I wouldn't want to evict you because of my pride. Maybe you think it would be too embarrassing. I wouldn't want to be seen to have failed. Is that it? Do you think I would let you prance around my home, destroying my plumbing, insulting my staff, and disrespecting my wife so that I can enjoy being a patron of the arts? Do you? Come a little closer, you pair of clowns. Listen carefully."

And then, in a majestic, low voice that sounded like a lion's purr, Dudley Peterkin said: "I would die before I would force my wife to endure any more of this disrespect. I would die, Lucifer. *Die,*

Kandyss. Do you think that you can threaten me with anything worse than death?"

Silence reigned.

"Then get the hell out of my house. Mr. Hendrix will bring you your lunch, but not your dinner. You will not spend another night under this roof."

"Some patron you are," Lucian grumbled. "I come here with a fortune in art and leave with a collection of water-damaged canvases."

"And whose fault is that?"

"Doesn't matter. I should never have accepted your invitation."

"You know what?" Dudley's tone changed. He seemed to have been struck by an inspiration. "That's a tragedy. Let me offer you one last kindness. I'll buy the lot from you."

"You'll buy the paintings?"

"All of them. At least then you can leave with a little extra money in your pocket and the comfort of knowing that your art is receiving the attention it deserves."

"There are forty-two canvases," said Lucian. "Forty-three including the one I completed last week."

"Forty-three. How much would you value the collection at?"

"A quarter million. Easily."

"Two hundred and fifty thousand?"

"Easily. That's a bargain."

"I'll give you eight thousand for the pile."

Kandyss attempted a derisive laugh.

Lucian said nothing.

"Cash," said Dudley.

"Cash?"

"Cash."

"Why would I take so little?"

"Because your paintings are bad. It took me a while to see it, but you've known the whole time, haven't you?"

"Cash?"

"Cash."

Lucian must have nodded at some point, because I heard Dudley open his safe.

"There," said Dudley.

"Fine," said Lucian.

"Get out."

Amelia and I were safely back in our respective offices when the Tremblays spilled into the hallway. Gradually their footsteps and the hisses of their whispered conversation faded away. Amelia stepped back out of her office. Dudley Peterkin stood with his back to her, his hands in his coat pockets, staring down the hall after the rogues.

"Dudley?"

The man of the house turned and beheld his lovely wife with the glowing eyes of a warrior recently returned from fending off encroaching hordes. "Amelia!"

I closed my office door. As I returned to my desk, it suddenly occurred to me that the issue of the stolen antiquity had not been resolved. I wondered if Dudley was going to call the police. It seemed unlikely to me that the Tremblays would bring it up again.

That afternoon, Liam and I were called into the East Wing by Lucian.

"We need a hand carrying out the bags," he said. He pointed to a mountain of suitcases and garment bags. I wondered if we were expected to fit it all into their sedan.

"Do you wish us to carry art for you again?" I asked helpfully, feigning ignorance of the conversation I had overheard that morning.

"No," said Lucian darkly.

"No," said Dudley, emerging from Lucian's studio with two canvases in his arms. "I've taken care of that. This is the last of them, Lucifer."

"Great," said Lucian, watching my employer leave. He turned back to Liam and me. "Just the bags," he said. "Come on. Let's go."

Kandyss appeared at that moment, attired regrettably. She looked as though she had been crying. One look at us set her off, and she threw her arms around Liam with a congested snort. "Oh Liam!" she wailed.

Liam looked at me over her shoulder, his eyes wide. His lips formed the word "help."

"Thank you for everything, sweetie!" she cooed. She kissed his cheek.

"Come now, Mrs. Tremblay," I said coldly, "goodness knows where that boy has been."

"Let's go, Kan," said Lucian.

The four of us managed to lift all the luggage, and together we waddled outside to where the Tremblays' car was parked. A second car, a taxicab, was just pulling up behind them.

"What's that for?" Lucian wondered aloud.

"I asked Liam to order it for me," said Kandyss.

"Why? We still have this car until tomorrow."

Kandyss shook her head. "I'm not going with you, Lucy."

"Really."

"Really."

"That's perfect," growled Lucian, watching as his wife started stuffing her garment bags into the back seat of the cab.

Liam and I silently helped the couple separate their belongings into the two cars.

"Lucy!" Kandyss squealed suddenly. "Look at him!"

We all turned from the task at hand and followed her gaze.

A wild and wonderful sight greeted us on the front lawn of Number Two Harper's Lane. Dudley Peterkin had been busy constructing a monumental edifice. It towered roughly twice his height, utilising the same architectural principles as a house of cards. In place of playing cards, however, were the paintings of Lucian Tremblay.

The architect of this abomination was standing back and admiring the work. In his right hand hung The Painting.

"What's he playing at?" Lucian snapped. "Did he just buy them so he can disrespect them? Typical."

From where I was standing, I was able to see a large, red jerry can tucked away in the bushes that lined the drive. Dudley's ominous purposes became plain.

"Do you know what he's doing, Lancaster?" Kandyss asked.

"Like you, I can only speculate, Mrs. Tremblay."

"And?"

"And I never speculate."

Swearing like an artsy little sailor, Lucian resumed packing the car.

"Time to go," said Kandyss. She drew in an immense breath that made her chest heave like a winter sea and released it as a loud sigh. "It's over," she said. She seemed to be waiting for Lucian to offer her some kind of reaction. I don't know if she expected him to cry or beg or shout, but he gave her nothing. He didn't even look at her. Resigned, she turned to Liam and appeared to be contemplating another farewell embrace.

I stepped in front of my underbutler. "You're quite right," I said. "It's time to go."

She looked at me morosely. "I won't forget you, Lancaster."

"It is kind of you to say so, ma'am."

She got into the cab. The three of us watched as it pulled out and rolled away down the drive.

"Done," said Lucian. He rested his wrist on the roof of the car and sneered at me. "I guess that's that."

"So it seems," I said.

"I never liked you," he said.

"No, sir."

"You're a hell of a snob."

"If you say so, sir."

He shut up and regarded me long and hard. I did not avert my gaze. He seemed on the verge of saying something but closed his mouth firmly, his lips pursed. He drummed his fingertips on the roof and climbed into the car.

Then he climbed out again. "I did want to say that I thought about what you said about your job."

I wasn't sure if this was an apology or not. It wasn't structured like one. "I see," I said.

"I can't stand you, Lancaster. You're not my type of guy."

"No, sir."

"But I appreciate how you think about your work. I'll give you that. You make it sound good to… to… well. Screw it. You know what you said."

"It is a privilege to enjoy the dignity of doing work well," I said.

He gazed at me wonderingly. "Wow, I hate you."

"Yes sir."

His door slammed. I stepped back and took up my position next to Liam. We watched the man fussing with his phone and seatbelt. He looked as though he was swearing angrily to himself. The car started and slowly eased forward.

"Mr. Peterkin means business," said Liam.

I looked up and saw that Dudley had set The Painting on fire. He was holding it at arm's length and watching the paint blister and blacken. He heard Lucian's car drawing nearer along the drive and turned to observe its approach. He waved with his free hand.

Lucian rolled down his window. "You're an idiot!" he roared.

Dudley grinned and tossed The Painting toward the canvas tower. A column of flame leapt some twenty feet into the air. He stepped back and put his hands on his hips, watching the inferno as it made the world a slightly better place.

"Impressive," said Liam.

"Yes," I agreed.

"Do I still have a job?" Liam asked.

Liam Hendrix no longer had a job.

The presence of the Tremblays had been the only reason for Liam's employment in the first place. Now that they had vacated the premises, his services were no longer required. The Peterkins allowed him to stay in the warden's cottage for as long as he needed while he interviewed for other positions. I made some phone calls personally and secured him the position of underbutler for a good family in Guangdong.

On his last day in the house, he thanked me for the brief time we had spent together. I thought this was gracious, considering how quickly I had been obliged to let him go.

"I learned a lot," he said, offering his hand.

I shook it warmly. "I'm pleased to hear it, Mr. Hendrix."

"Are you going to miss having the kid around?" Hoffman asked me that evening.

We were sitting in the library of the East Wing. The restoration of our beloved haunt had occurred without ceremony. Once the East Wing had again been shuttered, we resumed our habit of meeting there for drinks and TV without a word being spoken about it.

I poured Mr. Hoffman's beer and passed him the mug. "Yes," I said, "and no."

"Good to have everything back the way it was," said Hoffman.

"Precisely, sir. Mr. Hendrix is a very promising young domestic, but this household does not want what it does not need."

"Well said," said Hoffman. "Turn on the screen."

I found the remote in the writing desk and turned on the set. “It’s good to be back in here,” I said, pouring my own beer.

“Yes,” said Hoffman. “Now what’s that nonsense on the TV?”

“I think it’s a war documentary. About Korea.”

“Who needs it. I saw enough of this kind of thing to make my own documentary. Switch it to something good.”

I put on *Operating Groom,* an unapologetically terrible hospital drama.

Within minutes, a nurse on the screen was revealing her love for an impossibly unlovable patient.

“Oh hell!” groaned Hoffman gleefully. “What’s she thinking?”

“Love makes fools of us all,” I said.

“What’s she doing now?” Hoffman cried.

She was telling the patient that he was being taken off her list and they would never see one another ever again. She was also crying.

“What nonsense!” said Hoffman.

The patient, who had been declared permanently paralysed from the neck down only two episodes earlier, rose to his feet.

“A miracle,” I muttered.

“A miracle!” cried the nurse.

“What garbage!” said Hoffman with a grin. He proffered his mug. “Cheers, Lancaster.”

I touched my drink to his. “Cheers, sir.”

A knock sounded on the door before I could drink.

“Oh, go away,” muttered Hoffman. “Turn up the volume, Lancaster.”

I muted the television. We looked at one another expectantly, waiting for another knock. "Sir, would you like me to see if someone's at the door?"

"Is someone at the door?" Hoffman shouted.

The door swung open, and Amelia peeked in at us. "I'm sorry," she said. "Am I interrupting?"

"Yes!" said Hoffman.

"Not at all," I said, awkwardly setting my beer down and hastening to rise.

"Stay!" said Amelia quickly, stepping in. "You're off duty, Lancaster. Stay." She took a seat across from us.

Hoffman and I glanced at one another.

"What do you want, Amy?" Hoffman asked gruffly.

"I just wanted to chat with you both for a moment," she said.

"Oh yes?" I turned off the TV screen.

"It's so dark in here," Amelia said.

"We were watching our show," said Hoffman.

"Yes. And that's part of why I'm here. I just… I feel like I need to apologise to you both on behalf of Dudley and myself."

"Then why isn't Dudley here?" snapped Hoffman disagreeably.

"Well," said Amelia in a diplomatic tone, "Dudley thought that what I'm about to say would make Lancaster uncomfortable."

"So you'll make him uncomfortable all by yourself?" asked Hoffman.

"I'm sure I appreciate the consideration of you both," I said, "but really, Mrs. Peterkin, there's nothing between us that might warrant an apology."

"It's kind of you to say so, but I just keep thinking about the whole mess with the Tremblays, and it makes me feel bad. You were both so inconvenienced. Especially you, Lancaster. You got bitten and everything. Even this, the room that you and Dad enjoy relaxing in at the end of the day, was taken away from you."

"Quite right," said Hoffman.

"And we see now—not just me, Dudley really sees it too—we see that it was all a big mistake. A terrible, terrible idea that we should never have entertained. We won't do anything so rash again, and we're awfully sorry for how you were put out."

Dudley had been correct in believing that this heartfelt speech would make me uncomfortable. I squirmed in my seat, itching to stand, itching to straighten something. I glanced at Hoffman and could see that, for all his bluster, he was nearly as uncomfortable as I was.

Amelia rose to her feet with a sudden, sprightly movement. "Well!" she said brightly. "That's that. I just needed to say it. You get back to your show now." She walked to the door and turned to bestow a parting smile on us before leaving.

"Wait," I said suddenly. My voice was sharper than I meant it to be.

"Yes, Lancaster?" Amelia sounded surprised.

"Would you kindly turn up the lights, Mrs. Peterkin?" I asked.

"Lancaster!" hissed Hoffman. "What are you doing?"

Amelia obliged me. "How bright?" she asked.

"All the way, if you please." I sat up and adjusted my waistcoat. I had undone my shirt's top button, and I now concealed the fact by pushing up my tie.

"There you are," said Amelia.

"Thank you, Mrs. Peterkin," I said. "Perhaps you would like to sit down again?"

But Amelia was frozen in place. Her face wore an expression not unlike one who has just seen a ghost. She pointed to the small table that Hoffman and I were using for our drinks.

"But that's..."

"Hang it all, Lancaster," growled Hoffman.

On the table, flanked by our mugs of beer and well-illuminated by the ceiling lights, stood the stone tablet of Roman Law. Its frame of brass gleamed, and the large Latin letters seemed to spell out our guilt.

"Where did you get that?" Amelia asked.

"Found it," said Hoffman with the plausibility of a desperate liar.

"It's a long story," I said, "but the essential truth is that we had it stolen."

Amelia returned to her seat, but only perched on the edge of it, as if she might get up and fly from this den of thieves at any moment. "You had it stolen," she repeated.

"Yes." I could not make myself look at her.

"By that young man. The one you caught in March."

"Smart girl," growled Hoffman.

"That's why you were such idiots when the police were asking for his description."

"Yes," I said. "We had his telephone number from when we caught him in March. It didn't take much to convince him to take it from the Tremblays. We offered him cash and assured him that if he were caught, we would be entirely responsible. I left the veranda doors unlocked that night, and I told him where to find it."

"But why?" Amelia asked, her forehead creased in bewilderment.

"Had to do it," said Hoffman unrepentantly. "To break the bloody siege."

"What siege?"

"They were bullying you and Dudley," said Hoffman. "We needed to get the shooting started. Something that would get Dudley off his ass and start him swinging."

"Whose idea was this?" Amelia asked. She was a little bit angry now.

"Mine," I said quickly.

"Hold on, Lancaster!" cried Hoffman in genuine indignation. "It was no more your idea than it was mine!" He turned to his daughter and tapped his head proudly. "Not the first time your old dad had to think outside the box, Amy."

"I wish you hadn't," said Amelia.

"If I may," I said, "it did seem like the thing to do." Amelia looked at me expectantly, waiting for me to explain further. Taking a deep breath, I did so: "I had observed that Mrs. Tremblay regarded the tablet as symbolic of her own inadequacies. Mr. Tremblay, for his part, seemed to reinforce the idea. Forgive me for saying so, Mrs. Peterkin, but I believe they both resented you. Your concerns about the tablet's authenticity did nothing to dampen their jealousy. They were extremely defensive in their posture on this point. I felt certain that if the tablet should go missing, the couple would quickly come to the conclusion that you had something to do with it."

"Aha! So should I thank you for framing me?"

"Their belief was fundamentally an irrational one," I said gently. "There was no way they would communicate themselves winsomely in defending it. I had hoped to give Mr. Peterkin an opportunity to be unequivocally outraged by the Tremblays. I felt that hearing them accuse you of theft would give him just such an opening."

"Setting him up for a clean shot," said Hoffman. "That's what it was about."

"Seems a substantial gamble," said Amelia stiffly. "They could have pressed the matter further."

"Perhaps," I said, "but I did take care to ensure that Lucian Tremblay wasn't too self-assured going into the confrontation."

"Dare I ask?"

"I took the liberty of hinting to him about the real reason his studio was flooded."

"Oh, you did."

"I had not intended to, but the day before the robbery was scheduled, I had an interview with him. He seemed too sure of his role as the injured party. I felt that taking some wind out of those sails would make him more vulnerable in the succeeding bout with Mr. Peterkin."

"And how were you so sure that Mr. Peterkin was going to fight Lucian?"

"He and I had words the same day," I said.

"What words?"

"I cannot say. Mr. Peterkin saw fit to suspend our professional relationship temporarily so that we might speak confidentially. Man to man, as it were."

"Oh really."

"Yes. I believe that it may have galvanised your husband, ma'am. He seemed to gain some clarity on the state of affairs."

"Then why didn't he do something about it that day?"

"He still seemed unsure of how he ought to act."

"So you arranged for your young friend to steal the stone tablet that night."

"Yes, ma'am."

"So that they would accuse me of stealing it."

"Yes, ma'am."

"So that Dudley could get really mad."

"Yes, ma'am."

"And then you were there in your office to make sure I could listen to him tearing into them."

"I really felt that you would be sorry to miss it, ma'am."

Amelia set her hands on her knees and looked at the floor, thinking. The room was ominously quiet. Hoffman and I exchanged a quick glance. We were both feeling the tension of the moment.

"Mrs. Peterkin," I said, "would you like us to dispose of this tablet in some way?"

Amelia looked at me and then at the stone tablet. She rose once more to her feet. She stepped across to our table and touched the stone. "It's not real, you know," she said quietly.

"Just as you say," I said.

"Keep it," she said. "Keep it as a trophy. You've both earned it." She leaned down and kissed her father on the head. "Good night, Dad."

"Good night, Amy."

She stood next to my chair and kissed my forehead with the same fondness as she had her father's. "Thank you, Lancaster," she said.

I smiled. I was still smiling when the door closed behind her.

"Pleased with yourself, are you?" Hoffman snorted. "You didn't have to do that, Lancaster. She didn't need to know."

"A man must answer to his conscience, Mr. Hoffman."

"Fine. Just warn me next time your conscience is going to start issuing orders. Give a man time to take cover."

"Just as you say, sir."

I turned the show back on, and we let the matter rest.

I was putting the beer mugs in the dishwasher when I heard footsteps behind me. They were light steps and moved at an easy gait, almost skipping as they approached.

"Miss Schopenhauer," I said, shutting the machine and turning to her. "I would have thought you had left a while ago."

"Amy and I got talking," said Paige. With a light hop, she sat herself on the counter. She was smiling knowingly.

"Is that so?" I folded my arms and regarded her with some suspicion. "Talking, was it? And drinking?"

"Maybe."

"So unprofessional," I said in mock reproof.

She tilted her head to peer at me over her imaginary spectacles. "Oh really, Mr. Lancaster!

Where were *you* just now? Watching TV and drinking beer alone?"

"That relationship has unique dynamics of care," I said.

"Hypocrite," said Paige.

"I hope not."

"Amy told me what she found in your little library."

"Ah."

"Yes. I was very surprised to hear that our Mr. Lancaster had decided to meddle in the personal affairs of the household's family like that. Surely us domestics serve best when we serve within boundaries? Isn't that what you believe? Isn't it what you write in your diary every night? Isn't it printed on the inside of your glasses frame?"

"You exaggerate."

"Hypocrite."

"How much did she tell you?"

"Everything."

"I doubt it."

Paige cocked her head. "Why is that, Lancaster?"

"I just doubt it."

"She told me that you had the stone tablet stolen and that you set it up so Dudley would fight with the Tremblays and save the day."

"I see."

"Is that everything?"

"It's everything I told her."

Paige leaned forward, her mouth hanging open. "There's more?"

And perhaps I shouldn't have said so, but I did. I said, "Yes," and hopped up on the counter next to her. I took a tin of peppermints from my pocket and handed it to her.

"Is my breath that bad?"

"Not at all," I said with my best Errol Flynn smile, "but my story is that good."

"I'm nervous," said Paige. "You're making me nervous. What did you do, Lancaster?"

"Well," I said, "we should go back to the beginning."

"You as an infant?"

"Nothing so antediluvian. I'm talking about in March, when this whole business started. I was optimistic at first and had no desire to interfere in my employers' affairs. I was even curious about what life might look like with an eccentric artsy couple in the house."

"How about a Barbie and a sleazebag?"

"Miss Schopenhauer, please."

"Sorry."

"Pretty soon it became apparent that I, like the Peterkins, had left myself open to substantial disappointment."

"When did you know?"

"At that first luncheon. I saw things I did not like."

"Such as?"

"She put ice cubes in her chardonnay."

Paige pinched my arm reprovingly. "Ghastly."

"I thought so. That evening, when we caught that burglar snooping about outside the house, Mr. Hoffman and I saw that he had great potential usefulness. We took his number and set him free. We didn't know how he would come in handy, but there was something promising about his petty character and willingness to trespass."

"Sounds like a great guy."

"No. Detestable. He knocked me down the stairs, remember."

"Poor Lancaster."

"Initially, Mr. Hoffman and I were chiefly conspiring against the Tremblays on the grounds that we wanted to be reunited with our library. We were a displaced people, an exiled nation. Even our plotting had to occur in all kinds of conspicuous and awkward locations about the property. One time we were very nearly joined by Mr. Hendrix, just as we were about to pull the trigger on the robbery."

"Did Liam know any of this?"

"He did not. I have no interest in corrupting so promising a young man."

"So what did you do then?"

"Initially, we waited. The Tremblays were rapidly making themselves obnoxious to the point of offense, and we hoped we would be able to keep our hands clean. I thought the events of the art show would be enough to illustrate their incompatibility. Then I got bitten by the dog. I rather thought that would be enough, but it was not. Mr. Peterkin was at once both firm and gracious. The ideal ruler, perhaps, but his sending the dog away instead of the Tremblays was a disappointment. The time had come to look for opportunities."

"And what did you find?"

"Mrs. Tremblay asked me to have her bathroom cleaned daily."

"Of course!"

"I offered to clean it on Tuesdays."

"Oh Lancaster, what did you do?"

"On the last Tuesday that it was mine to clean, I found a terrible bathrobe lying about. I wasn't even sure what she expected me to do with it. Then, all at once, I saw the light. I stuffed the horrendous thing into the bath's drain and sabotaged the control for the water."

"Lancaster!" Paige's eyes were gleaming with delighted revulsion.

"Well, I did."

"I don't believe you."

"It's perfectly true. I don't know anything about plumbing, but I pulled it apart and took out a few bits that looked important."

"So when you and Liam had to go rescue Kandyss, you knew perfectly well that something was going to go wrong with her bath?"

"That's right."

Paige took my arm and a peppermint. "Go on," she said.

"I told the Peterkins about the mess she'd made. I told them about the damage to the bath's controls. They took it all in without great alarm. I wondered how many nuisances it would take before they became fed up. Was it even possible? But then, Miss Schopenhauer! Then Mr. Tremblay opened the door to his studio, and we saw that the extent of the damage was greater than we had intended."

"Oh, you didn't mean for that to happen?"

"Certainly not."

"Good to know there's a limit to your malice."

"Give me a peppermint."

"Say please."

I said please.

"When did you decide to steal the tablet?"

"We're not there yet. The next moment of inspiration struck when Mrs. Tremblay was complaining to me about having to use bathrooms without south-facing windows. I suddenly remembered that hers was not the only such facility in the house."

"Oh no, Lancaster."

"Our efforts in this campaign were twofold. We wanted the Tremblays motivated to leave, and we wanted the Peterkins motivated to evict them."

"So you told Kandyss to use the Peterkins' bathroom?"

"I didn't tell her to use it. I just planted the seed. I described the bathroom and its virtues until her eyes glistened with tears of desire."

Paige pinched my arm.

"And," I here waved my hand in a grandiose gesture, "the rest is history."

"I can't believe it!" Paige cried. "I feel like I don't know you at all!"

"Some desperate times demand that one be a man of action," I said grandly, picking a pill of lint from my trouser leg. I was feeling a very little bit silly. Maybe I had enjoyed too much beer.

"But was it really necessary? Couldn't you have just let Nature take its course? Wouldn't Amy and Dudley have ended up kicking the Tremblays out anyway?"

"Eventually, perhaps," I conceded reluctantly. "However, Miss Schopenhauer, it is worth noting that people are perfectly capable of living in a misery of their own making for years. There is no guarantee that they will start making the right decisions simply because they are unhappy."

"I still have questions."

"You need but ask them."

"You say that your initial motivation was getting your library back. Was that the only reason you did all of this?"

"Oh yes. I am fearfully petty."

"I don't believe you."

"Your skepticism this evening is positively disheartening. Did you have other questions?"

"What did you say to Dudley?"

"Just some words of wisdom. The kind that men of action murmur in low tones to one another on the eve of battle. Just that. Standard-issue manly murmurs. Low ones."

Paige pinched my arm again. "Tell me!"

"I can't remember exactly. Bracing stuff."

"You're lying. You do remember. You're just not telling me." Paige removed her arm from mine.

I felt the estrangement of our limbs quite keenly. "Well, there was one line that really got his blood going. I looked right at him, and I said, 'Mr. Peterkin!' and he said 'Sir, yes sir!'"

"Oh, he called you sir, did he?" Her arm was back in mine, and my heart was full.

"I am doing my best to recite a pre-battle murmuring, Miss Schopenhauer. Such things are not normally recounted for sport."

"Go on."

"So then I said, 'Mr. Peterkin! Sometimes even kind men and diplomats must accept risks for the sake of those they love!'"

"What did he say?"

And then I remembered what Dudley had said. He'd looked at me like he knew my mind and said, *"Kind men, diplomats, and butlers, Lancaster?"*

All at once, I felt all the silly go out of me, and I became sober once more. I straightened my glasses.

"Lancaster?"

"I think that perhaps I have allowed myself to be a bit indiscreet," I mumbled. I lowered myself from the counter.

"Where are you going?" Paige dropped to the floor next to me.

"I think I should retire for the evening. Good night, Miss Schopenhauer." I made for the back door.

The night air was cool, and the grass was already wet with dew. I inhaled deeply and gently swore at myself. I raised my chin and started crossing the lawn toward the bright light that illuminated the steps of the cottage. I could hear crickets and birds. Somewhere in the tall grass near the pond to my right, I could hear a bullfrog loudly broadcasting his own virility.

Then I heard my name, "Lancaster!" and I turned to see Paige standing outside her kitchen door, her arms crossed.

"Hello," I said softly.

"Hypocrite!" she snapped. It was the third time that she'd called me that in the past hour.

"I beg your pardon?"

"Telling Dudley that he needs to speak hard, frightening truths."

I said nothing.

"I don't believe you did all that just for the sake of an armchair in a library. You fought hard for the Peterkins. You put aside all your aloofness and professional discretion for the sake of something that really matters to you. I didn't think you had that kind of thing in you, but you do."

"Yes?"

"Well?"

"Miss Schopenhauer?"

"Can you think of any hard, scary truths that you'd like to name at this particular moment?"

I bowed my head and slowly walked back across the wet grass toward her. When I reached her, I saw that her eyes were becoming red. Her hair was down, and it tumbled about her shoulders in a torrent of silver-streaked copper.

"Miss Schopenhauer."

"Mr. Lancaster."

I could not think, so I started talking instead. "Sometimes, Miss Schopenhauer, it takes greater courage to stay silent than to speak a hard truth. Sometimes it would be an act of selfish cowardice to do that which terrifies one. For example, there might be a boy who loves a girl and is shy as anything around her. It might seem that bravery would be telling her... you know... the things that boys tell girls: that she's the most beautiful bit of creation he's ever seen; that he thinks about her constantly; that it's the mere thought of her that keeps the shadows of his perpetual loneliness at bay."

"Yes," said Paige hoarsely. "Those kinds of things."

"But then the boy looks in the mirror, Miss Schopenhauer, and he's not a boy at all, is he? He's an old man. He's an old, stick-in-the-mud man who will work as a domestic until the day he dies. Then he looks at the girl and sees that... well... she's nearer being a girl than he is being a boy. She's beautiful and has this vibrancy just flowing—cascading!—from her every pore. And the boy puts away his love letters and his roses and he sets out to do something much more difficult and much more terrifying. He accepts the reality that even if it would be brave—so brave!—to tell that girl how he feels, it would not be kind."

Paige took my hands in hers.

"Come now," I said. "Let's not get carried away."

"Mr. Lancaster," she said. "Please stop talking."

And then, without another word spoken, we got completely carried away.

Acknowledgements

I want to thank my editor, Rachel Starr Thomson. Not only did Rachel add a good deal of polish to this book, but she was also obliged to teach me a good deal about writing. She didn't quite have to introduce me to the alphabet, but it was a near thing.

Made in United States
Cleveland, OH
02 June 2025

17461811R00142